C000085738

Born in 1968, Peter Black has lived in London for most of his life. He graduated in Arts in 1992 and has, ever since, had quite a tempestuous working career as an estate agent, a restaurateur and an art dealer. Writing fiction has been, however, his one true passion all along.

Peter Black

THE BUDDHA OF QUEEN'S PARK

AUSTIN MACAULEY
PUBLISHERS LTD.

A CIP catalogue record for this title is available from the British Library.

ISBN 9781786125606 (Paperback)
ISBN 9781786125613 (Hardback)
ISBN 9781786125620 (E-Book)
www.austinmacauley.com

First Published (2016)
Austin Macauley Publishers Ltd.
25 Canada Square
Canary Wharf
London
E14 5LQ

'I want that job.' Read a sign in Kilburn jobcentre.

'You see, that's the general attitude you should have,' said the personal adviser, pointing at it. 'You should be eager to get a job. But I don't see that written all over your face right now, I am afraid!'

The man's armpits were soggy, and so were Ritchie's, although less evidently. He had put on his best white shirt for the interview, or rather the best of the worst, as he didn't want to come across as a well-heeled bum, but a needy one instead. To be fair, he had a smarter set of clothes, including his loud floral shirts and flashy mustard-yellow or burgundy pairs of trousers, the summery linens and cottons, the wintry tartan checks, the country gent black coat and his tailored navy-blue overcoat – which made of him an entrepreneur on the spot, whatever else he'd be wearing underneath – but those were no apparel to wear at a formal interview. They were only okay for unwinding, for fun time, for the girls.

The man sitting in front of him looked quite professional, surely less scruffy than the average jobcentre underling, his eyes were green, starey, and respectably screened by square-shaped lenses. He was reassuringly corpulent, brown-haired, and brisk.

'I don't work for the jobcentre,' he went on explaining, and then a moment later: 'I am on your side,' he added.

Ritchie was tempted to say: 'peace and love,' and simultaneously raise the two-fingered victory sign, but he didn't. 'I have no hard feelings,' he said instead, accompanying words with an ecumenical spread of both hands, the sort of gesture a saint might have pulled off instants before performing a miracle. But chances were there were going to be no miracles today, at this interview, only the usual bundles of recriminations fired at each other across the front line of the desk that kept them apart.

'May I ask you, how do you spend your spare time? Because you must have a considerable amount of it,' said the adviser.

'I meditate,' Ritchie owned up. 'Since I have been out of work I converted to Buddhism,' he said affably.

'That is an honourable thing to do,' the man said, 'however, as your work history lacks information, you are pretty much unemployable.'

Silence underlined the utter truth of the statement, the crudeness of it, its suppurating rawness. Unemployable, someone who can't be employed. Well, if he can't, there is not much to do about it, isn't it? Buddha, too, was pretty much unemployable, Ritchie thought, employment must have been the very last thing on his mind. 'What you think, you become,' the spiritual leader had once said, and so it was probably after he had been thinking about it with rare intensity that he had managed to attain such a high status of unemployability. That could be said of both of them, the master and the disciple, Buddha and Ritchie, united against employment and employability, may the force be with them.

6

'Your CV could be improved by adding casual work experiences, or even IT courses you have attended, to bring it up to date, make it more poignant,' the adviser went on. 'If you want, I can find employment for you as a salesman in the space of two weeks,' he volunteered.

'Thank you so much!' Ritchie yelped, 'only, I am not too sure it would work out given my new lifestyle... I mean, sales and Buddhism are not a match made in heaven, are they?'

The interviewer looked on sternly. 'Well, if this is what you really think then I am not going to give you a new appointment to help you out with career moves,' he said at last.

Ritchie nodded, disappointment digging a furrow right between his deep brown eyes, knitting his brows gloomily and comically close together, spoiling the suaveness brought to his face as a result of the enlightenment he had achieved, not without difficulties, after months of introspective probings.

As soon as he was out of there he started texting Sheila. 'Hey, what's up?' he began. Minutes elapsed before an answer came through. 'Hi, just chilling at home,' she returned.

'How come, no work today?'

'Nope, it's my day off.'

'Smashing! Wanna come over?' he ventured.

'What have you got?' she asked, 'you know what the conditions are.'

'I have a full-bodied, oak-aged, vanilla-flavoured Rioja, a couple of bottles of Marques de Montino. You can't go wrong with Montino.'

'Sounds good,' she chipped in. 'Although I'd say I am everything but vanilla when it comes to pleasures of the tongue.'

'I have everything your tongue needs,' he boasted. 'You coming then?'

'Okay, at the usual time?'

'Yup, I'll be waiting,'

'Be there at one.'

Sheila was neither particularly attractive nor too bright, pretty average in all respects, maybe even a touch below average. She was one of those ghost citizens comfortably ensconced in a well-to-do London suburb, draining the resources of well-to-do, abidingly well-established and clearly visible citizens, material citizens, weighty ones, not of the same ectoplasmic substance she was made of. She had gotten used to be overlooked anyhow, to being looked straight through, as if she wasn't there, had never been, and would never be. In theory, she wasn't even supposed to be living in the country. The last time she had popped into the Home Office to extend her visa, they had withheld her passport. 'We must do routine checks before you can have it back,' a stiffly, wan, and bespectacled clerk had sung. Plus she had to bring copies of her auntie's bank statements. They needed to make sure someone would grant for her, someone financially sound. Auntie hadn't been happy about it, not a bit.

'These are my savings of forty years,' the old biddy had cried. 'Why should I let them poke their noses into them? I have worked all my life, this is hard-earned cash, it's my money!'

'It's just to let them know that we aren't broke, that we got something to live on, if we are to stay in the country.'

'We? Why we? Have you slaved from Monday to Friday to put together this stash? Or I did?'

'I am just saying...'

'What are you going to do to pay me back for this?' Auntie had shrieked, looking away, as if the sight of Sheila were too horrifying to behold, as if she wished she had never taken her into the house, the stupid, lazy good-for-nothing.

'What do you want me to do, auntie? Tell me, and I'll do it!'

As a result of all the shilly-shallying and of the additional squabbling interspersed with it, she was late.

'I had to run a few errands for auntie,' she sputtered when Ritchie yanked the door open.

'I was about to open the wine,' he blared.

'Don't you dare!' she said, finger-pointing frantically.

He grabbed her index finger, tugged her in, and shut the door. She settled on to the sofa and he went to the kitchen to sort out the pouring ritual.

Half an hour and two small glasses on, she was already tipsy, loud, and much warmed up by the Marques de Montino. Ritchie's grey, tapering trousers had been swiftly disposed of as a superfluous, hindering and worthless pair of tubular rags. They lay lifeless on the armchair, beyond the gulf of his bumblebee-yellow lounge. His underwear had soon followed, and being grey too, had effortlessly blended with the pants, flopping right next to them. He stood up. She grabbed his left buttock and pulled him closer, then, raising the half-full glass, dipped his cock into the wine and drank the celestial nectar from the swelling appendage.

'Mmmf.' She went on moaning as soon as she had had a mouthful of him.

In all honesty it must be said that he had already given her other attractions a go, all ways in had been tested, tried, trodden upon at leisure, but of all the orifices, none seemed to fit him to such a degree of perfection as her

9

mush. Therefore, their lazy afternoons had ended up being a feast of degustations, fine wines and milkier overflows, keeping her highly engaged and him thoroughly entertained for at least a couple of hours.

'I have a new job,' she gave out after tea time. They both shuffled on to the kitchen after the first round of fun and frolics and he served her a hot brew, mango strawberry and banana infusions, pomegranate and raspberry, lemon and ginger, peppermint tea, religiously downed on a shower of salted peanuts and honey roasted nuts.

'What job is that?' he inquired.

'I am working as a clerk in a hardware store,'

'How exciting!'

'It's only part-time, easy-peasy stuff. All I have got to do is hang around and stick price labels on.'

'With the machine?'

'Nope, they don't have the gun, I have got to do it by hand. If nothing, I get the chance to flaunt my cool handwriting.'

'Yeah, right! You do those fancy flourishes at the end of each number? Price tags for eccentrics and the refined, the cream of the building site!' he japed.

'Hey, say what you like, the job is a breeze, and pays for my rent, or at least for some of it.'

'How about the till? Don't you serve the customers, too?'

'Nope, the till is off limits. They don't let me anywhere near it.'

'I see. They are afraid you might be tempted to tip yourself every now and then, when they're looking away.'

'Maybe. Anyway, who cares?' she said with a well-timed shrug of her shoulders.

Later on, around six, Ritchie's tummy took to groan and grumble. There's nothing so wearisome as drinking wine on an empty stomach, it saps all one's energies, it slowly consumes one's vital fires, to exhaustion, and hunger is just one of the inexorable consequences of it. He gave signs of impatience, rolled his eyes, as she kept blabbering on. He was definitely trying to let her know that time was up, and she must get lost.

'I am gonna go to Ladbroke Grove,' Sheila interposed after a pause spent in deep thought. 'To that Malaysian canteen, to get my laksa, yum.'

'Why, can't you go home to have dinner?'

'I am homeless,' she blurted out.

'How do you mean?'

'I mean auntie is gone out, and I don't have the keys.'

'You're saying you pay the rent to live there and she doesn't even give you a spare set of keys to the place?'

'Yup. She even takes the router with her when she's out and about, so no browsing for free.'

'What a harpy!' he chimed in. 'Well, good luck with your laksa then,' he added, seeing her to the door. 'See you soon,' he said at last, waving goodbye on top of the stairs as she was about to cross the threshold.

'You bloody Nazi!' Sheila muttered, then she was automatically thrown out by the door closer.

Ritchie spent the next ten or fifteen minutes tidying up the flat, a spot of vigorous hoovering was what his sitting room needed after the turbulence of their rather intense afternoon of heated debate and casual mingling. Once order had been restored, he microwaved his ready-made meal, chips and Swedish meatballs, wet with another glass of Montino, the last one, he vowed, otherwise he'd wake up to a throbbing hangover in the morning, and that was the last thing he wanted. After dinner he plopped himself back on the sofa and played some trashy music videos, in the hope they'd infuse him with renewed verve, striving to get back the energies devolved to prolonged and back-breaking fellatio.

When some of his pep had been recovered he grabbed the phone and dialled mum's number.

'Hello,' mum's sleepy voice answered.

'Hi mum, already in bed?'

'No, not really, only dozing off in front of the TV.'

'Yeah, that's what TV is for,' he sentenced judiciously. 'Look mum,' Ritchie went on, 'I need a little incentive, a pecuniary one,' he pitched.

'Again?' Mum replied, her heart skipping a beat. 'We just gave you four hundred quid. What have you done with it?'

'I had bills to settle, mum. It's gone, like the wind,' he said, blowing air through his tubed lips to dub the malicious hurricanes that had scattered away the cash, wholly against his will.

'We haven't got unlimited funds, you know.'

'How about Josh?' he went on. 'How is he faring?'

'Your brother is working hard to look after his family, he is been ill,' mum regretted.

'Ill? How?'

'A strange fever got hold of him. Doctors weren't able to establish what it was exactly, every few weeks he was running a temperature, and you ought to know by now how worryingly high his fever soars. Well, to cut the long story short, it turns out he has a staphylococcal infection.'

'Has he?' Ritchie butted in. 'Is it dangerous?'

'If the noxious bacterium is not defeated, he'll have flu symptoms more and more often, and he can't even afford staying home, with two young children and his

12

wife busy all the time taking care of them, he simply must go to work.'

'Mustn't he?'

'Yes, he must. However, on a positive note, the four-year-old boy is coming up just as lively and boisterous as your brother was, and the little girl is a joy to watch growing.'

'You see mum,' Ritchie cut in, 'their place, you said it was gonna be ours, didn't you?'

'Sure, that's what I have always told you both, that house belongs to you and your brother, fifty-fifty.'

'Cool mum! But he is the only one taking advantage of it right now... I mean, before he married, we used to rent it out, now that he lives there we are basically making no profit on the place.'

'Uhm, and what would you like him to do about it? Move out to help you make a profit?'

'Surely not, that would be harsh. Only right now it doesn't feel as if we are sharing fifty-fifty, but more like that he is taking everything for himself, that's all!'

'Josh is your brother, your own flesh and blood, don't you understand? When I and your father will be gone he'll be the only person on the entire planet that you will have left. It's just the two of you, is that clear?'

'Okay, mum, but I wouldn't want to have to suffer just because he's got married and has a family and I don't. Not only I didn't get the chance to do well, I must also miss out on what's mine, too. This is how I see it, to be honest.'

'How much do you need?'

'Even just a couple of hundred quid will do, for now.'

'Fine, you'll get it.'

'When?'

'Before the end of the week.'

'Love you mum,' Ritchie sang out.

Mum hung up. He went back to the kitchen, to retrieve the matches from the bits-and-bobs drawer, and striding into the sitting room, bent over the coffee table to light up the scented candle – a peach-perfumed one – and a couple of additional tea lights of plain white wax. Finally, squatting in the centre of the sofa, as if he were settling down slap-bang in the middle of the universe, and comfortably propped up by the two cushions that nestled one at each end of the sofa, and which he promptly seized for the just cause, he took to breathe, deeply, in and out, mindfully, inhaling the very essence of life, clearly pleased and reinvigorated by the flux of oxygen flooding his lungs and his whole body, and almost feeling the benevolent, beneficial rush of his bloodstream. Joining hands he said aloud: 'May I be well, happy, and peaceful; may I be well, happy, and peaceful; may I be well, happy, and peaceful...' Those words seemed to have indeed a soothing effect on him, from the start. As soon as they were pronounced, the consonants and vowels that constituted the very fabric of the formula wafted gently all around him, spreading well-being, and he could distinctly make out the amount of positive energy released during the prayer.

After a while the mantra embraced creation as a whole. 'May my work coaches be well, happy and peaceful; may my parents be well, happy, and peaceful; may my relatives be well, happy, and peaceful; may my friends be well, happy, and peaceful; may the indifferent persons be well, happy, and peaceful; may the unfriendly be well, happy, and peaceful...'

At last, when the litany ended, he added: 'om mani padme hum,' which means hail to the jewel in the lotus, and helps to achieve all the qualities necessary for a rebirth in the pure land of Buddha at the time of death. It is also said of those who recite it, that as soon as they are immersed in a body of water, the water is blessed for the contact, and that their descendants, up to the seventh generation, won't be reborn in the lower realms. The rapturous ritual was rounded off with the enunciation of his profoundest good wishes: 'Through the virtues I collect by giving and other perfections, may I become a Buddha for the benefit of all,' Ritchie phrased eagerly.

In the morning, around eleven, the phone rang. He had just stepped into the shower and given himself a quick rinse when the gadget started vibrating and chiming tunefully. 'No way!' Ritchie cursed, and just as he was, dripping wet, hurried out of the bathroom and grabbed the squirming mobile.

'Yes, who's there?'

'Hello, is this Mr. Richard Barker?'

'Yes it is, I mean I am, it is I, me,' he burbled.

'I am calling regarding your application for the admin assistant role at Tripodium Ltd. My name is Rona Lewis. May I ask you a few additional questions before we take you further in the selection process?'

'Of course you can.'

'Wonderful. Are you looking for full-time employment?'

'I am indeed.'

'What are you doing at the moment?'

'Erm, I was about to shower...'

'What I meant was, are you employed these days?'

'Oh, sorry, well, not really, at least not entirely.'

'So, would you be willing to start with us right away?'

'I would, yeah!'

'Excellent! And what makes you think you would fit the bill?'

'Uhm, yeah, I am very well-organised, punctual, and reliable. Have you read my CV?'

'Yes, I have,' Rona piped.

'Good, I am all those things that are written on it, then!'

'Lovely! We want to invite you to come in, today, this very afternoon, to have an informal chat with our managing director,' the secretary informed him.

'The managing director? Cool! Yes, I can do that,' Ritchie confirmed.

'At three o'clock, would that suit you?'

'That's absolutely fine.'

'I'll email you all the details in a jiffy, address and so on.'

'Smashing!'

'Please be on time,' Rona pleaded, 'and dressed in formal attire.'

'I will, no problem, thanks!' he said, and pressed the red button.

At ten past two Ritchie strode majestically into his favourite betting shop on the high road. It would be helpful to mention which agency he had actually picked, because in all honesty the high road had almost exclusively been taken over by bookmakers and estate agents, with the rare, albeit compulsory, exception of intermittent food outlets, dealing in either cooked foods – world foods, for the record, the Middle and Far East being proudly and vigorously over-represented – or in the usual supplies for the average, penny-saving household. The bookie he frequented, the one he had elected, over the years, as his personal office and invaluable trading place, was an exuberant feast of dark blue, dark-blue sign, dark-blue carpet, and dark-blue seats. In Ritchie's opinion it suited well the professionalism expected by businessmen from every walk of life. Other premises were candidly bathed in white and nationalistically topped by red friezes, or uniformly painted green, evoking pastures and expanses trodden by saints, adventurers and travellers, where luck was meant to dwell in overflowing abundance. But none of it made sense to him, blue was the colour of transactions, exchanges, undertakings, and ventures, the predominant colour of the twenty-pound note, the colour of the sky, the future was blue. Dotted with the green of the turf, in regular swathes that striped the screens on which destinies were made and unmade, fortunes promised, flashed, proffered, speedily suggested and just as quickly denied, taken back, procrastinated.

'Hurry up!' cried Artan, 'the two twenty race at Windsor is just about to start.'

The chap was impeccably dressed, as always, in anthracite grey blazer of the straightest and plainest cut, if only a tad tight, and trousers of a darker shade, edging toward black, but slightly too short for his scrawny legs. They gave him marked chaplinesque airs, although he was no tramp. His black hair appeared even blacker in virtue of the vast amount of gel he oiled it with, making a striking contrast with the rosy-red of his cheeks and forehead.

'Who's the favourite?' Ritchie boomed.

'Shenanigans,' Artan said, 'seven to four,' he added, raising a two-handed seven digits followed by a single-handed four in the face of Ritchie. Then he went on tapping the side of his nose with his index finger. 'It stinks!'

'It does, doesn't it?' Ritchie said, curling his upper lip. 'Look at him, he can't even get into the stall, the bugger.'

Shenanigans was, in fact, giving the jokey a hard time, no matter how insistently the jockey patted him on the lustrous neck and how firmly he encouraged him, digging in his heels in the animal's flanks and whipping its muscular rump. At last the horse was driven in, the gates blasted open and the race began.

'Go my son,' bawled an Oriental-looking man of undefined age, albeit overall on the youthful side, as soon as the wild bunch took to gallop at full tilt. 'Go my son, go my son, go my son,' he kept yelling, his eyes riveted to the screen. 'Go my son, go my son, go my son...'

It was all going quite well for the Irish thoroughbred, then the overstretched, ebony neck of Moonwalker, the horse running second, caught up with him. They were only yards away from the finish line, flying head-to-head, breathing hard.

'Go my son, go my son...'

Moonwalker was apparently going much stronger. Chances were he was going to make it, yes, he was.

'Go my son, aaargh!' wailed the Chinaman, tearing his slip over and over again, until the shreds were a cascade of confetti scattered at his feet. Shenanigans had come second.

'I told you it stinked,' said Artan.

'Yeah mate, it stank!' Ritchie agreed, congratulating him for the timely tip-off with a pat on the back.

Half an hour later Mr. Barker and his Kosovar pundit were poised to break the bank, to rock the house, shaking it from its foundations. They were primed and set for success.

'Check this out, buddy!' ejaculated Ritchie as soon as the beast they had picked to stake everything they had on – about a hundred quid each – jogged out of the stables and was ridden triumphantly through the passage leading to the paddock.

'Flipping began his two-year-old career in a one-mile maiden race at Newmarket on soft ground,' Artan read from the *Racing Post* while his comrade gazed at the screen. 'He broke slowly, and was held up by jockey Tim Quince before making headway two furlongs out.'

'Impressive,' Ritchie spewed.

'He led inside the final furlong and ran on to win comfortably by half a length from Jon Jones' Ishmael,' Artan added. 'Five weeks later, Flipping ran in the Tom Frazier Condition Stakes over seven furlongs at Doncaster. Only two horses threatened to oppose him, and he started at odds of one to two. Quince tracked the leader Diamond Bling before spurring Flipping to the front a furlong from the finish. The horse darted past his opponents and pulled away to win by thirteen lengths, in impressive style.'

'Smashing!' Ritchie butted in.

Minutes before three o'clock the race started. The pacemaker, Reuben, jumped right ahead, setting a fast and furious pace and immediately opening a considerable lead by half-way. Flipping was asked by jockey Tim Quince to go after the leader and successfully passed Reuben shortly after the three-furlong marker, going on to open up a lead of six lengths on his chasers with two furlongs to go. Ritchie and Artan were on the edge of their seats, their hearts racing just as tumultuously as their star horse. They gaped at the screen with half-parted, dry lips, their lives were brought to a standstill for a bucketful of interminable seconds. However, in the final furlong twelve to one shot Zoltan began to make up ground, increasingly, getting frighteningly close to Flipping, storming in, and flanking the favourite, who was soon only a nose ahead. On they flew to the finish line, where such was the perfect alignment of the two horses that nobody could tell who the winner was. Slow motion replays were shown, over and over again, then the verdict came in. Zoltan had taken the first place, followed by Flipping only fractions of a second behind.

'This is flipping crazy!' thundered Ritchie.

Artan was speechless, benumbed. Their hearts had plunged to unfathomable depths upon communication of the final result. Ritchie's mobile suddenly rang, it shook in his pocket. He pulled it out.

'Hello?'

'Hello, Mr. Barker, it's Rona here.'

'Oh, Rona! Is everything okay?'

'We were wondering by what time you will be in? We were supposed to meet at three o'clock...'

'Indeed,' said Ritchie, 'I am on my way, Rona. It'll only be a matter of minutes, I am stuck in the traffic. Tell the managing director I'll be there soon!'

'Fine then,' Rona said.

Ritchie hung up, and checked the phone number from which the call came. It wasn't unknown, no, luckily it showed on the display. He scrolled the options menu and selected: block this caller, then swiftly pocketed the phone and gave Artan the mournful look only a loser can exchange with another, equally dejected loser after the cruellest double debacle.

One week on Ritchie had another appointment at the jobcentre, with yet another adviser, Mr. Delroy Williamson. Williamson was an Afro-Caribbean chap of undefined age and ponderously wide girth. At a first glance one had the distinct impression he was ballooning out of control, just as well as for long-lived tree trunks his age could be determined by studying the phenomenal evolutions of his ever-expanding circumference. He had been assigned to Ritchie to monitor all his movements. His customer had been unemployed for too long for the Department of Work and Pensions not to have any doubts about him. How could he possibly get by with the hardships of living in metropolitan London with his meagre income? Foul play might be involved. So Williamson had to keep close watch on him, probe him, test him weekly, make sure he wouldn't slip out of the net the brainboxes gravitating in the high spheres had cast to gather up all the unruly and ungovernable of the realm.

'How is the job search going?' Williamson asked.

'It's going quite well,' Ritchie replied.

'Have you had any interviews?'

'Yes, to be honest I have.'

'How did it go?'

'Well, I am still waiting to hear from them. You see, they interviewed me over the phone, they asked me lots of questions about my current situation, my future goals, and about what drove me to apply for the position advertised... Then this secretary said I could be okay for the role, only she needed to talk about it with the managing director, then she'll let me know.'

'Very good!' Williamson praised, his hands folded on the desk in a business-like posture. 'My manager has advised me to sign you up to a course, it's a two-week programme which will give you access to IT services, in order to refresh your skills. In other words, it's an opportunity to attain gainful employment, at no expenses. We will refund your travel costs, all you have to do is bring in the receipts and I will personally issue a payment straight to your bank account.'

'Thank you so much!' Ritchie whinnied.

'You will be notified shortly when the course starts, and where to go, by text message,' the adviser added.

'Fine, I'll be looking forward to it!'

Before the end of the week a text message popped up on the screen of Ritchie's phone. It read: 'please attend the course induction on Friday the sixteenth,' which made sense. Unfortunately, the month the text referred to was the one already gone by. Ritchie couldn't really see how he was supposed to attend this induction on a backdated Friday. He texted the sender to get some additional information, an explanation perhaps, but his message didn't elicit any response. He just forgot about the whole episode. Then, two weeks later, when summoned again by Mr. Williamson, Ritchie was asked why he hadn't joined the course as agreed.

'Look,' he said, showing the message safely stored on his phone. 'They gave me the wrong date, plus there was no address. What was I supposed to do? I did text back, but got no replies!'

Williamson picked up the phone anchored to his desk, wearily, and dialled the esteemed course organisers.

'Mr. Barker here says the details he was sent were wrong, well, actually they are wrong. He just showed me the message you texted him.'

Awkward silence, and a baffling suspension of credulity followed, and right after that, the routinely checks to ensure that no such error had occurred. But as a matter of fact it had, there was no doubt about it. Now the incredulity gave way to the apologies. Ultimately, Williamson was told they'd send a new message, this time with a date set some time in the future rather than in the past.

'I am really sorry about this Mr. Barker, it's all been an innocuous misunderstanding,' the girthy adviser antiphoned.

'Will my payment be delayed or stopped?' Ritchie mooched anxiously.

'No, it won't, as it wasn't your fault, the money would have been withheld only if you had refused to take part to the programme.'

'Phew, thanks a lot!'

'I would be delighted to spend the evening in your company,' said Lady Davina.

'I am thoroughly up for it,' Ritchie rejoined. 'I hope you don't mind me being not that much into exclusive relationships.'

'I suppose we should see how it goes,' she chimed in.

'Sure, let's do that!'

'Perhaps we could rendezvous somewhere around the Royal Festival Hall. Does that suit you?'

'It does indeed.'

'What time?'

'Shall we say, six o'clock?'

'Yes, six is fine. Message me as soon as you'll arrive.'

'Will do.'

He spent a good half-hour digging stuff out of his wardrobe to find a pair of trousers that would fit the occasion, something not too bold or too fancy, neither he wished to turn up in drab grey chinos though. At long last he fetched a pair of blue moleskin slacks that was just about perfect for the tricky juncture. However, having kept them dangling for months unworn from a hanger, the legs were cut in half by a whitish line, a narrow, shallow groove opened by the horizontal bar into the cloth by the sheer pull of gravity. He muttered a couple of curses, tried to brush off the marks imparting a gentle stroke with his hand, unsuccessfully, then wondered if a splash of cold water from the tap would help. Having wet his fingers, he gently massaged the discoloured creases until, to his elation, there was no more trace of the white lines.

When he rolled in on the Station Parade, the hands of the big clock up on the facade announced with the acutest of angles that it was half past five. There was plenty of time, Ritchie surmised, to reach the South Bank. Unfortunately, the folding gates of the station appeared to be drawn halfway over the threshold, and that was a bad omen. In fact there were no trains running, a handwritten board informed, and a bus parked a short distance away had its doors open and idled, waiting for passengers to step on. It was the railway replacement bus, deployed to cover the tract that had been shut down due to maintenance and upgrade works. The evening hadn't got off to a good start. Minutes later, while bottled up in a long queue at the traffic lights admitting to the Cricklewood Broadway, Ritchie took to prod nervously his phone's tiny keyboard: 'Are you going to be there at six o'clock sharp?' he asked. 'There's a little problem with trains here, I have been diverted,' he explained. But there was no answer. 'Oh, well,' he thought, 'let's just wait and see!'

As soon as the escalators spat him out of the abysmal depths of London Underground, he strode and stared furiously ahead, hurrying in an intimidating straight line, as if he'd wish to say to casual strollers and passers-by milling around: 'Get out of my way, I am late!' In the end he was only eight minutes late. Lady Davina was pacing the well-scrubbed alley lying like a plush grey runner between the row of bars and restaurants and the Royal Festival Hall, when Ritchie climbed to the top of the stairs. As soon as she spotted him, she glided swiftly forward and, unfolding her arms in a welcoming gesture, rushed to meet him, kissing him on both cheeks.

'I feared I'd never make it!' Ritchie said, panting.

25

'It's okay, don't worry, I haven't been waiting long,' she reassured him.

They sauntered toward the river and down the ramp, under the Golden Jubilee Bridges, marvelling at the clemency of the weather.

'It's just a touch chilly, but we are extremely lucky that it's not raining,' his date opined.

'Sure,' he reckoned. 'It is quite mild, compared to the blustery last few days.'

'I gather you are an entrepreneur of some sort, aren't you?'

'Indeed that could be said of me,' Ritchie confirmed, 'even though the measure of my profits might not be impressively overwhelming. In other words I don't make as much money as I ought to. I am not broke, but I am not well off either.'

'My husband, as well, is trying to go solo. Of course he is at least twenty years older than you, or thereabouts, and has had already a fairly distinguished academic career, but he is always keen on pushing the boundaries of creativity,' Lady Davina put in gently. 'Being affluent is not all there is to life,' she remarked. 'One needs personal achievements, and some satisfactions on a deeper level, to be fully accomplished.'

Ritchie nodded, every now and then throwing quick glances down at his interlocutor, whose stature was several inches shorter than his, allowing for a bird's-eye view of her slouching posture, and for the occasional peer at the general conditions of her neck and of her vee shaped neckline, where her skin told the tale of her ageing in capital letters, or else in zigzagging lines and sudden wrinkling, especially when she twisted her neck to meet his gaze. As for the lines on the legs of his trousers, Ritchie contrived to squint at them, too, nonchalantly, to ensure they'd only be visible to himself, who knew exactly where to find them, other than that, the velvety lustre of his blue moleskin slacks, matched with his white shirt, his grey cardigan and his black raincoat, exuded feelings of pure luxury and well-being.

'When he left me, only a few months ago, I was in shock,' Lady Davina owned. 'It will take quite a while to digest our separation.'

'Yeah, I suppose it must have been a hard blow.'

They had veered off the river bank promenade now, steering into the cobblestone-paved gardens lying in the shadow of the Wheel. She hesitated somehow, then said: 'Shall we walk back east? Find something to do or somewhere to go?'

'Yes, why not?' he granted.

'Ever since his departure the house has been so empty, and cold,' she resumed. 'I drift from one room to another in utter despair. Everywhere I look, every nook and cranny is steeped in memories, every object reminds me of him, of a lifetime of tender love and care, which now is only a reminiscence, as if it were all just a dream.'

She had taken him on a path parallel to the glorious and ever-crowded riverside, past side roads depleted and silent, in bewildering contrast with the noisy hubbub soaring only yards away, alongside the Thames.

'My workplace is not far from here,' Lady Davina said, pointing to her right-hand side with a languorous gesture, whereas her index finger was never actually raised above all other digits, but they were all directed together at the cluster of buildings where, approximately, her workplace was. 'I teach very young children. It's a wearisome task, a tough assignment, but also the source of many little daily gratifications... We should perhaps return to the well-trodden route,' she mused at last, realising they had been trudging through obscure backstreets for quite a while now.

Once they had regained the main path, and as the lady's outpour of emotions approached steadily its climax, Ritchie couldn't help thinking of that other path, the one leading to enlightenment, and encouraging the faithful to develop two essential qualities: wisdom and compassion, often compared to a pair of wings that, fluttered together, enable the beneficial flying that comes with any spiritual journey, the sort of flying that lifts the spirit to higher regions more like. In the present case, he saw clearly, he was being called to exercise his compassion, to exert an active sympathy and a willingness to bear the pain of others, and to act selflessly, in order to alleviate suffering.

'May Lady Davina be well, happy, and peaceful,' he prayed innerly.

'To keep my job I have had to retrain and qualify on several occasions, well past fifty. Despite having lived most of my adult life in London, I have never acquired citizenship, only the right to reside,' she lamented. 'After all these years, though, I truly see myself as a Londoner, albeit an adopted one, and wouldn't dream of going back to Australia, at least not yet.'

Around Blackfriars Bridge the commotion intensified. By the time the Millennium Bridge stretched in full view – an unsteady, floppy gangway held by slingshot-shaped supports rather than a solid, wind-resistant platform, that's how the bridge came across – Ritchie and Lady Davina had begun weighing the possibility of a pit stop for refreshments. Refuelling must be dealt with.

'There is a Lebanese restaurant just around the corner,' she proposed, 'shall we pop in for a snack? Do you like Lebanese food?'

'I do,' he replied. 'I am not fussy about food. As long as it's simple and the ingredients are genuine, it's fine by me.'

Regrettably, when they breezed in, the place was packed. On account of the wood oven, spewing flaming tongues of fire, the room was nearly as hot as a crematory chamber. Two corporate ladies were standing on the way in and having a chinwag, while waiting for seats to become available. Since Lady Davina surveyed the venue in search of somewhere to nestle, one of the two birds, a tall thirty-something blonde in business attire, gave her a nasty, belittling look. Apparently there was quite a good deal of leaning in the doorway to embrace.

'We should go somewhere else perhaps,' Lady Davina said.

Ritchie concurred.

In the end they opted for Wine City, a wine tasting destination not far from Borough Market, tucked in a discreet backstreet, under an arch, and away from the madding crowd. The main boozer was actually booked for a birthday party, a black, aged bouncer in black suit politely informed them, but they were free to make use of the adjacent wine bar if they liked. 'It is still part of Wine City,' the bouncer croaked, pointing at the double gate half opened on to a spacious patio.

At the counter a few sparks flew between Lady Davina and the Spanish girl who took care of their order. It was just a matter of seconds though, owing to a sort of linguistic misapprehension.

'How is this red wine?' Ritchie's date had asked the waitress.

'Erm, full-bodied... Erm... Wait please, let me just get the list,' the girl had stammered in a poor, guttural and rasping English. 'But you can taste it if you like,' she had blurted out at last.

'Yes, please, may I taste it?' Lady Davina said.

The dark-haired and curly girl had then poured a small measure of the Chilean Sangiovese in a large glass. The degustation was solemnly carried out, in spite of the waitress's utter lack of professionalism and abominable sloppiness.

'Mmm, yes, I think I like it!' Lady Davina sentenced.

'Could we have two large glasses of it?' Ritchie clinched.

The Spanish girl went on filling the crystal clear vessels up to the white line closest to the brim. Her sloppiness turning useful this time, since Ritchie's glass was topped up slightly above the mark. It was probably his reward for having kept neutral during the ladies' brief dispute.

'I went to see my mum recently,' said Lady Davina, once they had settled down in the patio. 'My heart was heavy, as I knew it could be one of the last times I saw her. She is well over eighty. The level of poisoning I had to endure was barely bearable, my brothers are smokers and they were constantly lighting up their cigarettes in the house. I am so glad you are not a smoker,' she added.

'Yeah, I used to smoke, to be honest. I quit a few years ago,' Ritchie said.

'The last ten years by my husband's side have been the hardest ever,' she cried, staring at him across the table. A waitress, most probably another Spanish, although a shabbier looking one, served them a plate of mezze. 'He has been taken ill, confined to a wheelchair, and the remedies of Western medicine seemed to have no effect on him, other than as painkillers.'

'I distrust medications myself,' he butted in.

'I began researching alternative cures, alternative medicine, like natural remedies from the Far East, such as acupuncture, to try and find a solution to our problem.' Lady Davina dipped the bread into a saucer filled with humus, then shot: 'My husband and I hadn't had sex for ten years, before we separated. Doctors told us it would be detrimental to his health.'

'I see. That's harsh!' Ritchie observed.

Yes, it was harsh,' she echoed, putting on a shawl and wrapping it around her shoulders to fend off the onset of shivers. 'It's getting chillier,' she said.

Their glasses were refilled one more time, and more helpings of bread were brought to the table, the triangle-shaped khamiris they had been served in the first place having proved not enough to scoop up all the dips.

When they were back on the Bankside, the wind was picking up. Lady Davina stood for a while near the parapet, taking in the stunning view of the Thames sprinkled with a myriad lights flickering into the night. They walked a little more, and as they traipsed along the stretch between the Globe and Tate Modern, she made another, sudden stop to gaze at the river. Then Ritchie kissed her. There's no running away when a woman decides it's time to kiss, she will put you right on the spot where she wants you, making sure her offer won't be spurned. Kissing went on for a minute or two, a whole volley of smooches were exchanged by the couple before their stroll would be resumed, and when it was, finally, resumed, she linked arms with him and on they sailed genially, like two pigeons in love.

Having made it to the National Theatre, the lovebirds swerved left without saying a word, as if kissing had muted their tongues, or else as if they didn't want to wash away the aftertaste left by those gentle, tentative pecks in a flood of superfluous wording. At the roundabout they prolongedly and cautiously looked right while waiting for the green man at the traffic light. Vehicles came down the curve unrelentingly fast. The London IMAX cylinder glowed bright and blue against the darkened sky, its giant display flaunted a bikini-clad model – bronzed by effect of her enviable, uniform tan – flying a fantasy-pattern pareo. In the station the escalators swallowed the couple back down into the underground clammy shafts of the tube. On reaching the bottom they realised they'd have to go separate ways.

Ritchie threw in: 'would you like to come to my place?'

It was a plain and simple question. The answer wasn't delayed long.

'Uhm, yes, why not?' Lady Davina said, and so they both boarded a northbound train.

Of course there was still the little hitch of the railway replacement bus to settle, they had to come off the train a couple of stops earlier and travel the extra distance at a slow-paced tempo, queuing at traffic lights and turning in narrow residential roads, before being delivered to their destination. A brisk walk in the much-freshened air of the hour leading up to midnight, through tree-lined avenues and a section of the high road, took them to Ritchie's flat at last.

He poured some more wine, while she made herself at home on the bumblebee-yellow sofa.

'I am afraid I have only white wine.' Ritchie felt the need to apologise.

'Well, if nothing else it's chilled to the right temperature,' she observed, raising the glass.

Some more smooching, and fondling, was practised, and then layers of clothes were exfoliated. As soon as he took to bang her, Lady Davina pleaded: 'please be gentle, will you? You see, you are big and I am small.'

Ritchie heeded and relented.

Later on, when the amatory frenzy on the sofa had fizzled out, he invited her to snuggle up in bed. However, before long he regretted having done so, for Lady Davina activated her snoring loudspeakers in well under a minute. He lay supine and wide awake, his eyes lost in the dark, and took to ruminate on the events of the last few hours. At some point, when his brain sent him distressing signals, and the realization that he must pull the plug dawned on him, Ritchie tried a few moves to see if he could shake his bed buddy out of her snoring. He kicked his legs around, under the duvet, but it was all in vain, she kept on snoring and wheezing in the dead of night. He had to resign his hopes of rest. 'Well,' he thought, 'it's for one night only, and for compassion's sake, I suppose,' and learnt to endure light-heartedly the long vigil.

He must have fallen asleep at the break of dawn, and for a couple of hours only henceforth. Then Lady Davina woke up, and so did he, and they were at it again, rolling and petting each other under the sheets. Sometime later an unusually blazing sunlight broke in through the fissures in the blinds. Ritchie got out of bed and shuffled to the kitchen, where he started fiddling with cutlery and dishes. He served Lady Davina a hearty breakfast of coffee and honey-glazed brioches. While she was quaffing a honeyed brioche on the sofa her phone rang. It was her son, from Canada. A couple of minutes into the conversation her son broached the subject of an eventual get together.

'Oh, yes, we are not broke, are we?' she said, holding a half-chewed brioche in her left hand, 'I think I can afford the ticket, can't I?'

On she rambled for a good five to ten minutes. 'I am so sorry about this,' she said at last, putting away the phone. In due time the odd pair slipped back in their clothes. Lady Davina stole to the toilet to micturate, ablute, and to restore order to her hairdo. When she had done, he grabbed the keys from the coffee table and off they went to the station again, where the shuttle bus eternally idled and rared to go. Ritchie kissed her goodbye and watched her intently as she stepped on to the front door platform, before he'd retrace his steps to the flat.

On Sunday morning, in the Bosnia and Herzegovina Community Advice Centre, Artan and Idriz talked out the collection rounds of Uncle Tariq. Artan, as usual, was impeccably dressed, despite his customary ankle-high trouser legs. On the festive day he added a touch of further refinement to his outfits by means of a red or yellow knit lapel flower – most probably the woollen counterpart of a rose – today the bud was yellow. His hair was well-oiled as usual. Idriz, by comparison, looked like a delivery boy. He wore jeans and a white T-shirt at all times, whatever the weather, rain or shine, even in freezing cold temperatures, and his darker complexion and hair made it almost impossible to place him anywhere in Europe. The Community Advice Centre was a sort of club, a meeting point for all the refugees from the West Balkans, for all the tribes issuing from ethnic communities of Roma people dwelling in Bosnia and Herzegovina, Croatia, Serbia, Kosovo, Macedonia and Montenegro. Each region was well represented. Over ninety per cent of the evacuees to the UK from that particular area were deemed too scarred, mentally – as a result of the brutal Balkan war that targeted civilians en masse unmercifully – to be able to cope with their daily routines without a little help from the host country. Many had seen their family and friends exterminated, some had even suffered torture, rape, or other unspeakable ordeals, and the fact that they had been transplanted in a foreign land, with all the difficulties related to integration and to the learning of a new language, had certainly made their life no better, or, at least, no easier. Even those who had acquired British citizenship felt that they were all but fully consolidated in British society. Their Community Advice Centre was an ample, rectangular space topped by a moderate vault, just off the high road. They held assembly there, discussed the issues of the day, or quite simply flocked in to have a chat with fellow countrymen.

'He brought home a computer,' said Artan, 'main unit, monitor, printer, scanner, all the parts.'

'That's good!' spewed Idriz. 'Computer is good!'

'Okay, but the house is almost full up, there's no more room.'

'We are gonna sell a few things we don't need,' Idriz said.

Uncle Tariq's collection rounds were proving rather fruitful. The old geezer set out as early in the morning as he possibly could, sometimes as early as six or six-thirty. He donned his brown leather jacket, gave the grey, longish hair a vigorous brush and a backward sweep, and the grey, thick mustache a downward stroke, and off he went, dragging an ordinary shopping trolley, except that the actual luggage bag had been removed and replaced by a tangle of bungee cords coiled around the frame of the trolley, just in case he had to secure bulky items on his two-wheeler.

Thus equipped he went about picking up all the discarded appliances of the neighbourhood: kettles, toasters, irons, ironing boards, microwave ovens, blenders, electric heaters, lamps, hair straighteners, occasionally he'd stumble across the odd fridge or washing machine, and if they were small enough to be loaded on to his cart he wouldn't overlook them. Then of course he found wears, parkas and scarves, trouser belts, hats, ladies' derbies and bowknot bowlers, men's trilbies and panamas, or the more trivial woolly caps and gloves, which might as well be a hundred per cent acrylic rather than cashmere or merino, and yet they added a touch of warmth to any respectable wardrobe. He found shoes, too, oodles of them, all shapes and sizes and colours. Shoes for all seasons, for the whole family. No wonder at the foot of the towering plane tree shooting high up only yards away from the tribe's council house retreat there would always be at least one or two pairs of shoes dropped there overnight. Way too thick and fast was the input of footwear to be digested with ease, some boots or moccasins or open sandals, when supplanted, had to be ditched, albeit reluctantly.

All day long Ritchie had been trying to get back some of the sleep he had lost during the heated night of passion with his new flame. He had drowsed intermittently on the rumpled bed, and in the sitting room, or slouching over the kitchen table. But even those bits and bobs of rest he had so laboriously accomplished hadn't provided him with the enduring satisfaction he had been looking for. And once he had done with snoozing, his eyelids had still felt so heavy that rolling them all the way up had been nothing short of an Herculean task. Around five Lady Davina sent him a message: 'thank you for keeping me company.'

'I had a lovely evening,' he replied.

'Feel free to call me anytime you like,' she went on. 'Next weekend I am having guests at home, they will be staying the following week as well, then I'll be free again.'

'I will call you, no doubt!'

On Monday morning, shortly past ten, just as a pale, low sun beamed down the high road, like a sort of giant, artificial lamp pointed at the set of a suburban soap, Idriz, in familiar, bicep-enhancing, tight white T-shirt, nimbly carted the computer Uncle Tariq had seized pronto to the Cash Generator store wedged between the bank and an unbranded estate agent – the latest two in the long train of banks and letting gurus' premises sharing the stage with lowlier breeds of moneylenders and cheap retailers – main unit, monitor, printer, scanner, wires, plugs and loose ends, the whole shebang.

'Can I see a proof of address?' The girl in dark-blue chequered shirt bleated at the checkout.

Idriz produced a folded letter out of his back pocket and spread it open on to the counter. It was a notice from the council, the umpteenth benefit decision update bearing council employees' diligent calculations, what he was owed and what he owed, the second score amounting pretty much to an irrisory sum, and after all he and his clan had no tangible assets, or intangible for that matter.

'Can I see a proof of purchase?' The girl dug in.

'Purchase?' he mimicked.

'Yes, did you buy this gear?'

'No, it was a gift, donation!' he cried, drawing a capable box in mid-air with both his hands and gesturing as if about to tender it.

'Fine,' she said, 'if they are claimed as stolen we will get back to you, are you aware of that?'

'Sure, no problem,' he nodded keenly.

'I can give you a hundred pounds for the lot.'

'A hundred pounds is good.'

Just as the girl's plump, anaemic fingers were inching their way into the cash register to pinch the promised notes, Idriz swivelled two hundred seventy degrees around on his heels to have a good, panoramic view of the shop and its contents. The place struck him as an Aladdin's cave of the useful and the pleasurable. A

37

Dewalt portable cut off saw, a cordless screwdriver, an angle driver, an eighteen-volt drill kit and an impact-ready drilling set all gleamed invitingly in the window on his right-hand side – the Crown Jewels would have been less appealing to him as he gaped ecstatically – and a couple of electric guitars and a bass hung sinuously on the narrow wall adjacent the window. The left-hand side was instead a treasure trove of pocket-size gadgets and portable electronics, even these were shielded by a sparkling glass pane. Dozens of compact cameras, smartphones and older, not-so-smart handsets were lined up in double and triple rows, shoulder to shoulder with blingy wristwatches, DVD box sets, laptops, notebooks, music players, music recorders, card readers, film scanners and, last but not least, a sixty-one keys Yamaha digital keyboard with X-style adjustable stand folded beside it, bewitching Idriz with its neat juxtaposition of black and white bars.

Idriz teetered, pondered, weighed the alluring alternatives destiny had just fanned out on his very own path to aggrandisement, the fate of the tribe lay in his hands, however knotty or grimy they might appear to the casual observer. In the end he chose pleasure over duty, as any respectable epicurean would have done.

'How much is the Yamaha?' he inquired once he had swivelled back to face the counter and the girl.

'It's a hundred ten with the stand and headphones,' she said, 'but if you want it, it'll be a hundred, okay?'

'Okay,' he settled, 'it's a deal!'

That evening the excitement was palpable in the clan's retreat. Idriz's first lady, Adelina, struggled to contain the feverish mood that had gotten hold of the kids and made them scuttle about, engaging in reckless, wild chases, their shrilling shrieks barely able to keep up with the chiming cascade of soft notes freely flowing out of the living room piano bar. Just as well as Idriz was dark and reasonably jacked-up, his wife was, on the other hand, gracile and ghostly fair. Her hair fell in natural blonde waves, her twisted hoop earrings and her loose ponytail made her virtually identical to any other cockney gal – wasn't she from the East, too? The South East, for a fact (although not born within the sound of Bow Bells, but used to the harsher babel of daily shelling instead).

What a brilliant idea this had been, a sheer stroke of genius had set on fire Idriz's otherwise elementary mind when he had devised to take home some serious entertainment for family and friends, for the neighbours, for himself, for the advancement of the arts.

'Ain't no sunshine when she's gone,' he sang now, proudly standing at the keyboard of wonders. 'It's not warm when she's away...' Adelina, gazed languidly at her gifted husband as she leaned against the doorpost and clearly doted on him. 'Ain't no sunshine when she's gone, and she's always gone too long, anytime she goes away.'

A crowd of associates had spontaneously gathered in the bare living room. Sokol, Lavdrim, Dritan and Edonis had dropped by, also Ramiz, Milot, Liridon and Saban, Isuf, Gezim and his wife Mirjeta. They were all sipping cans of lager and tapping their feet to the rhythm of one hit after another as the evening grew darker, deeper, and more intense. Out in the front yard Uncle Tariq and blue-eyed, balding and grey-mustachioed Grandpa Andri – Adelina's old man and sole parent to have survived the apocalypse – smoked and drank cheerily. Not bad indeed for a Monday night.

When Ritchie walked back in the office, on Tuesday afternoon, before he would risk another ton on a straight bet, Artan, beckoning him over to the corner between the toilet and the fruit machines, began to stammer uncontrollably.

'It stinks, it all stinks to high heaven,' he said.

'What's new, mate?' Ritchie demanded.

'Finding a racehorse trained on the traditional hay, oats, and water regime would be nearly impossible,' the Kosovar read from a freshly unrolled magazine published by industry watchdogs and self-professed equine lovers. 'Many racehorses become seriously addicted to drugs when their trainers and vets administer them phenylbutazone and cortisonsteroids,' these last two words were amply mangled, 'to keep them on the track even though they shouldn't be racing at all. They pump them full of drugs, every day. When there is so much money at stake, those running the show will do anything to make their horses run faster.'

The two pals exchanged glances charged with a burning sense of disgust, the expose sounded like a rude awakening.

'Thousands of thoroughbreds are bred for racing every year,' Artan went on, 'depending on the country, only five to ten per cent ever see a racecourse. As for the others, unless they are lucky enough to find another career, they are disposed of, typically at a slaughterhouse.'

'Yeah, mate. That's what they stuff our ready-made lasagne with!' Ritchie screeched.

'Horses begin training or already racing even as their skeletal systems are still growing and unprepared to handle the pressures of running on a hard track at high speeds. Strained tendons or hairline fractures can be tough for vets to diagnose, as a result, the damage often goes from bad to worse at the next race or workout. Moreover, horses do not handle surgery well, anaesthesia can throw them in a disorienting state and they may easily injury themselves in the process. Again, in ninety-nine per cent of the cases an injured horse can only be put down, it is the easiest option, to spare their owners the vet fees. Even the horses sent to auction are almost certainly bought by middlemen acting on behalf of horse slaughter plants...'

'Enough mate!' Ritchie barged in, waving a hand as if to shoo away the poisonous venom the article was pouring into his delicate, discerning ears. 'That's enough grief for one day,' he reflected.

On a crisp Friday morning Ritchie was swept along by dribbling fringes of commuters, in the aftermath of the rush hour tide. He boarded a train heading north, three stations later landed on a half-empty platform, scurried down the wide, imposing staircase on top of which, like a temple resting on concrete pillars, the station sat, and hurried down the Olympic Way. At number one the revolving door whisked him in. He stated the reason for his visit to a brown-eyed and brown-haired receptionist wearing a light grey, satin top rather slack around the milky neck, her curves bulging out enticingly.

'This will be your pass for the week,' she said, handing out a clear plastic sleeve shielding a card that could be clipped to his breast pocket, had he been wearing a blazer.

Ritchie thanked her and put away the pass, then he was addressed to the lifts. He was hauled all the way up to the twelfth floor, strode into the hallway, past the door, and ended up before yet another reception desk.

'Your name is not on the list, Mr. Barker,' a curly, Afro-Caribbean secretary sang.

'Well, here is the message I was sent,' Ritchie said, showing the text with the details of the appointment, date, whereabouts and all.

'I see,' she muttered, and lowered her head once again on the bundle of papers piled up on the desk, to try and find his name among the others enrolled on the course. 'Perhaps you could just add your name to the list,' she resolved, holding out a biro and the sheet with the uppercase column names typed on it. 'That will do.' Finally, he was ushered in for the eagerly-awaited induction.

As soon as he set foot in room four, right at the bottom of the corridor, he realised there was no way he could squeeze past those already sitting down around the adjoined desks. The place was packed.

'Let this gentleman in, any of you, will you please?' Cackled a sturdy lady of African descent in a red top and black trousers.

Chairs were dragged forward in a couple of points, until Ritchie found a suitable passage and, gliding between the scraping chairs and the partition wall, headed straight for the back of the room, where he slumped dissatisfiedly down by the window.

'My name is Gloria,' the coach intoned, 'and I formally welcome you all to Sabrina Ronson Job Access. Here you'll be given an opportunity to acquire new skills, to carry out your daily job search, to exchange ideas and comments with other jobseekers and with us, your mentors and advisers.'

Stillness and speechless stares directed at her were the most immediate reaction to those opening sentences. She went on, undeterred.

'Feel free to use the college facilities, as long as you will do so in a respectful and thoughtful manner. In the kitchenette you can have as many coffees and teas as you like, you are welcome to bring your own food and to warm it or dish it up in the kitchenware available, or you can buy sandwiches and drinks from an authorised vendor, who will be popping in every day at one o'clock with his trolley, you will hear the bell announcing him. Classes will be held from nine to three thirty, please be on time, to avoid lagging behind, we have got work to do, unless you want to stay here some extra time to complete your questionnaires.'

Hands were raised, questions were posed, but Gloria dissolved any doubt whatsoever her skeptic audience might nurture. Meanwhile, the atmosphere in the stuffy room was getting too glutinous for Ritchie's taste, his powers of endurance were being critically tested, breaking point, he gathered, must not be too far away, a crisis loomed right ahead on his causeway to wisdom. As usual, when he found himself haplessly immersed in a hostile environment, when the murky waters of triviality and nonsense reached his waist, or soared even higher up, to his neck, if not, alarmingly, up to his chin, and mouth, inducing one of those anxious, interminable moments of sincere panic, during which he felt as if his most vital functions were about to be hindered or lethally delayed if nothing would be done to avert the worst case scenario, he retreated undetected in the ivory tower of Buddhist philosophy. How would the Buddha have fronted a similar plight? Surely he'd have lifted his spirit high up, to vertiginous heights, flying like a kite on waves of fresh air, or suspended like a bird of prey on beneficial thermals, floating into the aerosphere, under the azure vault of the limitless sky, out of reach, temporarily freed from the exacting weight of all that is worldly and mortifyingly onerous.

'I and all sentient beings, until we achieve enlightenment, go for refuge to Buddha, Dharma, and Sangha,' he chanted in his mind, once, twice, trice, fourfold, fivefold, and up and away he winged.

'You can go now,' he heard at last, from light-years afar. 'And remember, be on time on Monday morning!' Gloria was preaching, as the jobseekers stood and scattered at random to the four corners of the room before filing out.

That afternoon, upon letting her in, Sheila flounced into Ritchie's flat glowering at him and noticeably flustered. She flumped down on the bumblebee-yellow sofa, scowled some more, then rummaged in her bag, uttering a mild curse, until eventually she found what she was looking for.

'Here,' she gasped, producing an invoice with a blue heading and the logo of a cheap Philippine airline, 'I had already booked my one-way flight to Manila!' She wailed.

'What made you do that?' said Ritchie, putting down two wine glasses filled with Claret on the reclaimed teak coffee table.

'Auntie is driving me mad!' she replied, sobbing. 'She storms into my room to check me out, to see what I am up to, if everything is in order, to tell me to dust the place, to turn the lights off... Just imagine, I have to sit in the dark after dusk to read or watch TV!'

'That's hideous.'

'If I take a shower, I must wipe the whole bathroom squeaky clean when I am done, if I go out, I must do the shopping for her, before I can actually meet my friends... She is becoming a living nightmare!'

'Yeah, sometimes relatives can be annoying,' Ritchie added comfortingly.

'She is not even my real auntie,' Sheila warily got off her chest.

'Why don't you ditch her?' he insinuated.

She paused for a while, only long enough to take into account this last suggestion, and to give it some thought, however, pretty soon her maundering outburst was resumed, and a flood of new grievances issued through her carnose lips. Ritchie, eyeing her up from his favourite corner of the sofa, only inches away, had no other option than to put her mouth to better use.

Several mouthfuls later, her degustation having been carried scrupulously through, Sheila objected she was going to leave earlier than usual.

'I have got to see Rodney, we are going for a bike ride in the park,' she brought up. 'He hasn't been too well lately. He is down with depression.'

Rodney was her best, gay friend. He was a clean-shaven chap with a youthful demeanour, whom the retro tortoiseshell oval glasses made an eternal student. He was always neatly dressed in plain shirts and pastel-coloured crew-neck jumpers, and his brown, side-parted hair uniformly swept from left to right was the icing on the cake of his wimpier, geekier rendition of Clark Kent.

'He looks like a Colombian,' quipped Sheila, showing Ritchie a picture of Rodney she happened to have on her phone.

On Monday morning, since he had to get in by nine o'clock, Ritchie was a fraction closer to feeling the full force of the rush hour. All around him, faces that only minutes earlier had been probably animated with livelier expressions, were now willingly flattened down, reduced to a deadpan drabness that suited well the on-duty mode to which the working hours inexorably drew. He, too, in the general undertone of professionalism that pervaded those he went about joining, on the platform and, as soon as the train pulled in the station, in the car he had chosen, found impossible not to assume a similar, sombre posture, trying to focus on the day ahead just as though it were going to be as productive and financially rewarding as if he was heading for a brokerage agency in the heart of the City to trade on behalf of multimillionaire investors. He was in fine fettle. The black, waterproof overcoat added a pinch of style to his average-man look, as a result, none of

46

those who took notice of him would have ever imagined he was only a lousy unemployed, coerced by the state to attend classes meant to instil in him a higher sense of duty, to shake up his conscience and rebuild his atrophied work ethic, so to speak.

He was thirteen minutes late, not a big deal apparently. Gloria and the classmates were all still settling down when he darted in. She had wisely allowed for some margin of sloppiness, provided it would be a negligible margin. Soon the door was shut and the tutorial began in earnest.

'You will be required to perform written tasks. There will be a book of exercises to complete for each day,' the adviser grumbled from her desk, partially screened by her open laptop. At last the questionnaires were neatly piled up on Gloria's desktop, ready for take-off, and a beefy, turbaned girl who sat in the front row, volunteered to pick them up and pass them around. 'They are all very basic exercises,' Gloria reassured the jobseekers, some of whom were already deeply distressed even just after flicking through the first few pages of the book they had been handed over, as if the Codex Justinianus or a yellowed papyrus chock-full of hieroglyphs awaited sussing out. 'Don't worry,' she added in a raised, vibrant tone, 'I will help you overcome difficulties.'

The first day flew sluggishly by. So dull were the tutor's instructions and so penetratingly squawky the timbre of her voice that Ritchie had to resort to his indomitable willpower to avoid brainwashing of the worst kind and a potentially serious case of noise pollution. His eardrums ached, those hammering inculcations were rebounding inside his head, hurting his grey matter. Cells of vital importance were being mercilessly bombed, crushed, and brutally torpedoed. Barriers had to be hoisted to prevent annihilation. The sole point of interest in the room seemed to be to him – as he anxiously scanned the place in search of something peaceful to look at – the panoramic window running all over his left-hand side and letting in stunning views of north west London, the tube station, the tracks getting lost in the distance, the high road, the surrounding hills, and the houses, which were visibly spaced out in the outer neighbourhoods. Until at last, where the hills met the horizon, the signs of human presence were almost totally engulfed in a thick scramble of bushes, boughs and leaves, and the country took definitely over.

'Any chance they'll be giving you a job?' asked Janet Barker over the phone, in the evening.

'How should I know, mum?' Ritchie wondered. 'For the time being they are giving us some advice, telling us how to get a job, I suppose that's a start!'

'Is it? You have been getting plenty of advice already, I dare say, it's high time you were given a job!'

'Not any job though! I need a proper job, a permanent one, in the public sector more like, the last thing I want is to be whipped around like a muppet. I don't deserve that, do I?'

'Your father has been working forty years for a private company, nothing wrong with that!' Mum demurred.

'Back then things were slightly easier. I reckon, it wasn't such a mess as it is now.'

'Uhm, we had to work our way to retirement, believe me, it was anything but easy.'

'Okay mum, I'll give you that!'

He was bang on time for day two of the Job Access. Again, books were handed out – a whole new set of them – and Gloria, patrolling the stretch of carpeted floor that surrounded her desk and the short catwalk by the gloss whiteboard, soon after nine resumed her nasal drawl in the hope of injecting some of her enthusiasm into her demotivated audience. Ritchie stuck to his seat right at the back of the room, whence checking his phone and answering to the zillions of incoming messages could be done with very little disruption. Filling the questionnaires wasn't exceptionally hard, as far as he was concerned, plus their coach tended to meet the needs of the class in a rather accommodating fashion. Having synchronised the jobseekers' efforts on the page and exercise of choice, she set a time frame for the completion of each task. It could be ten, twenty minutes. Thirty for the most puzzling activities.

Once time was up, figuring out that not all of her students had provided the necessary answers – a simple look around would help her gain such revealing intelligence, or the occasional glance at the teetering expressions, the writhing and head scratching of those gravitating close at hand would suffice – she grabbed her blue marker and proceeded to jot down on the board the correct answers, word by word. All Ritchie had to do was idle for a while, engaging in cheeky and compelling online chats with virtual new partners, or else take in the atmospheric revolutions of the one-hundred-eighty-degree wide landscape unfolding to his left-hand side, and when, punctually, Gloria scribbled down the solutions, nonchalantly copy them on to his book. All it took to get out of trouble was a sort of primitive cut and paste job.

Unsurprisingly, his underhand tactics didn't go entirely unnoticed. Jason, a blue-eyed, ginger-blonde guy ensconced by the window, kept muttering allusions, in marked cockney accents, to Ritchie's skiving methods, which contrasted clearly with his own diligence and sense of urgency.

'I couldn't stare at a bloody screen for hours on end,' Jason said to Ali, an Asian boy who strived to reproduce his lilt, when he spoke. 'It would drive me mad!'

Ritchie didn't deem opportune to pick up the gauntlet. Wouldn't Buddha himself have praised the valour of endurance?

'Get a job!' Yelled Gloria just before lunch time, while everyone was quite busy peering at the laptops tethered to the desks, pretending to do job hunting. In fairness someone did get a job on day two, a girl in a headscarf. She had been sitting by the door and everything, from her desultory body language to her reluctance to speak up, had given away her unrest, she must be inwardly screaming she couldn't wait to get out of there. And in fact after lunch she was excused to attend an interview.

Gloria's tone of voice soared to unimaginable heights as the main aim of her tutorials – launching new careers – came into sight, only twenty-four hours after she had taken a new batch of applicants in hand.

She was warned, at the reception, during the lunch break on day three, that the chief executive of the welfare-to-work programme was about to pay a visit to the premises. He must be somewhere down there, on the ground floor, nearby the building, if not already in the basement, parking the car.

'Quick, get rid of this smelly food!' Gloria yelled at the turbaned girl sitting in the front row, whose cooperative attitude had gradually been replaced by a chilled stance, and whereas she had previously been up for channelling all her energies toward the absorption of the notions the adviser went about imparting, now she seemed to be wholly taken by her high-calorie McDonald's, which surely helped to justify her corpulent frame. She didn't take much heed of Gloria's tip-off anyway, and even though she gave signs of being willing to wrap it up, in the end she kept munching and golloping down undisturbed her Big Mac Meal.

When the break was over Gloria picked up where she had left off, contriving to carry on with her tutorials as if nothing out of the ordinary would be about to take place. However, soon the presence of the chief executive in the building was felt, he must be already haranguing the jobseekers gathered in room number one, and he'll be shortly breezing in. Ultimately, a loud, choral cheer from the room next door announced the boss's proximity. He was not alone, blue-suited and completely bald, the thirty-something executive was flanked by an equally blue-dressed chappy chap whose ash-blonde hair, albeit cut rather short, appeared to be escaping the curbing action of the comb, curling and waving way beyond the patching up power of the most careful grooming.

'Hello everybody!' The chief executive hailed in a joyful Australian twang, taking centre stage right in front of Gloria's desk – she acquiesced to be temporarily eclipsed. 'How are you finding the course?'

His enthusiasm didn't spark any corresponding strong feelings, as he had probably hoped, and so he went on of his own accord, waxing lyrical while enumerating all the plusses of an active participation to the work programme.

'Has any of you found a job yet?' He suddenly asked.

Immediately Gloria pointed at the headscarved girl who, after the interview – which allegedly had been successful – had been readmitted to the class, only for a few more days, until she would start working in her new role. The girl outstretched her right hand aloft, and the Australian executive promptly congratulated her. He invited her to share with the class her undeniably positive experience, and held her up as the quintessential personification of what Job Access was about and what it could do for the long-term unemployed.

John, a hirsute out-of-work builder in a moss-green fleece, dared to interject approvingly, to which the Australian, turning to face him, straightaway replied: 'Where are you from, John?' Having spotted the guy's name on his makeshift paper desk nameplate.

'Ireland,' John said.

'I guessed it from your accent,' the Australian returned. 'You see,' he felt the need to explain to the audience as a whole, 'even if we lose business when one of you leaves the course, we still want you to find suitable employment and get out of here as soon as possible. Yes, we want you to leave us behind and get out there, and be happy again! That's our aim, our mission, to make sure you are given an opportunity to show off your skills.'

Homily over, he introduced his sidekick, although upon getting in the driving seat, his coy associate made clear at once he was no second best. His way with words struck listeners at once, and mesmerised them, as he gestured, drawing shapes in mid-air with the right hand, wiggling and rotating fingers at ease and suddenly closing his fist when a conclusion approached. His first-rate education and privileged social background was evident. Despite his young age he cut a fine figure of politician in the making.

Soon after the main concerns of the organisation had been mapped out and reiterated, the Australian, recovering the hot spot, invited the class to express appreciation for what was being done for them at no expenses whatsoever. 'Let us hear your voice, give us a cheer and a round of applause!'

'Yeah!' The jobseekers shouted unanimously, blandly clapping, like a bunch of wet seals responding to the solicitations of a ringmaster.

Not long after the boss's exit, Gloria thought wise to inform the presents that the blondish, unassuming chap who had so fervently underlined the importance of a programme like the Job Access in the wider panorama of Britain's job market, was none other than Ethan Bloor, the eldest son of a former prime minister still very much involved in politics as envoy to the Middle East.

The same Ethan Bloor that years earlier, aged only sixteen – when his father had been firmly rooted down at number ten Downing Street – had been arrested for being drunk and incapable just a stone's throw away from the prime minister's residence, in the heart of the whirling West End, and merely days after the premier had suggested the introduction of fines on the spot for drunken and disorderly behaviour. An ambulance had been called, since the teenager was vomiting fluently on the pavement, and when taken into police custody, he had been giving a false name and age. However, after a thorough search his true identity had surfaced, and he was driven safely home.

'We were out celebrating the end of GCSE exams,' he had innocently stated upon regaining sobriety.

Mr. Bloor declared, in his own defence, that sometimes a father's job can be tougher than the prime minister's.

Nowadays Ethan was a happily married man. According to the headlines the wedding ceremony had been quite sensational, it had been celebrated in a picturesque country parish in Buckinghamshire, amid family and friends' best wishes and warm embraces and under the watchful scrutiny of the press and the paparazzi. As for his career choices, he had as many paths unfolding at his feet as Ritchie and fellow jobless colleagues had never even dreamt of. Now he was touted as the next MP for a constituency historically held by his father's party, now he was photographed while intently following the debate between prospective leaders of said party, the left hand propping up his chin in thoughtful raptness, at other times acting stardom was forecast for him. Flights of fancy aside, he had actually already been governor of a primary school in Westminster, and raised funds on behalf of a well-established bank, before gracing the Sabrina Ronson group with his quasi-decennial experience in management and business development.

'He is just a spoiled brat!' Sentenced Jason barely two minutes after the executives' surprise blitz.

'If I were you I'd curry favour with him,' said Janet when Ritchie mentioned the episode.

'And how am I to do that?' He snapped.

'By any means. Stick to him, be servile if needed, at least until you get what you want.'

'There's no way I can keep track of his movements though, he was in today by pure chance, who knows when and if he'll be around again.'

'Well, do some research, find out where he can be seen.'

'I might be taken in as a stalker, mum!'

'But you might just as well get an opportunity, too!' she retorted hotly. 'You never know what's in store for you, what's around the corner, and you'll never know if you don't try. You see, this could be a sign that things are about to turn around, maybe your moment has arrived.'

'Uhm, okay. Ahem... Mum?'

'Yes?'

'I have bills to pay... Could you lend a hand?'

'How much d'you need?'

'A hundred quid. That will do.'

'I'll tell dad.'

'How is Josh?'

'The fever is gone, but the staphylococcus hasn't been defeated yet. It is a tough customer, antibiotics don't seem to have any effect on it.'

'That's grim!'

'The doctor said your brother could be an asymptomatic carrier.'

'Is that bad?'

'Not if he goes on without being affected by the disease,' Janet summed up. 'You should see how lovely is little Jamie. He is so attached to grandad, your father adores him. Every time he buys him a new Lego set the boy says: "grandad I love you very, very much!"'

'That's swell.'

'Call him sometimes. It's not that hard! Don't tell me your hand is gonna hurt if you pick up the phone and dial Josh's number!'

'The hand is gonna be fine, mum, but the wallet might resent it!'

'A five-minute call, Ritch, how much does that cost? A pound?'

'It depends on what time you are calling.'

'Call him in the evening then.'

'I'll think about it.'

Less than a week after the buzzworthy piano bar night, Idriz and his clan found, among the various letters dispatched by the council to reassure them that everything was being done to make their sojourn in England as smooth and pleasant as possible, even enjoyable to an extent, a note from the Pollution Control Team; someone had lodged a complaint, not all of their neighbours endorsed musical talents and upbeat merriment as one would have expected.

One day on, in plain grey T-shirt and worn denims, Idriz queued from eight o'clock outside the Citizens

Advice Bureau, a low-profile shop space flanked by a colourful, eastern-flavoured grocery bazaar replete with fruit and vegetables displayed six feet away from the high road tarmac in sloping cardboard boxes, and by the hundredth letting agency – judging from the speed at which they mushroomed one could surmise all locals did was renting as main occupation, and gambling in the spare time.

At eight the queue was already long, despite the chill morning air and the touch of frost making the pavement slippery and edging forward treacherous. Although the windows of the Advice Bureau were clear such was the cornucopia of A4-sized leaflets, notifications and law updates pinned to the glass that having a peep inside was utterly out of the question. Nothing moved either, out there, during the long wait lasting till nine o'clock on the dot, when the sign hung on the main door was manually turned and the word closed was swiftly replaced by open, not a sniff of life, not a hint of activity could be detected, apart from the half-frozen line of dejected customers eager to be admitted in, letting one suppose there must be some other way in, at the back, for those who manned the outpost, or else that they must be inhumanely obliged to sleep on the premises, as a further proof of devotion to the machine of the state, that with unlimited generosity employed them indefinitely.

Idriz didn't mind the cold, on the contrary, it gave him a sort of positive shock, it infused him with a vibe that was anything but regrettable, with an electrifying injection of life. If Adelina's vaporous warmth and the children's boisterous fun hadn't brought him around yet, the biting whiffs gently sweeping the high road had the power to awaken all his senses. And then again, how paltry this vaguely windy, shady cold was compared to the icy temperatures of his native mountainside, take the northern winds away and the south east of England would be no different from the south of France, or even the Mediterranean perhaps, pushing one's luck.

The Bureau opened its door to the citizens at last, in they orderly filed, slightly benumbed after the long wait, and in dropped Idriz, giving his generalities to the receptionist – whose desk was just about wide enough to lay a couple of sheets of paper and a pen or two over it – and thereafter flumping down on a chair in the parlour, grasping his ticket. One by one the customers were summoned in the appropriate room, where the right kind of advice, and possibly help, would surely be offered. Time ticked by, ten, twenty minutes, half an hour, even a whole hour perhaps elapsed before the number printed on his ticket flashed in red on the electronic display, next to the number of the pertinent office. He stood up, waded through a narrow and dim corridor, swerved past an open door to his left, and was invited to sit down again, in stammering tones, by an Afro-Caribbean lady in her forties, in professional attire – black gown and stripy, adherent shirt. The cubicle was hardly bigger than his bathroom, at home – which wasn't any bigger than any other terraced house bathroom – one window let light in from a backyard, a barred window, in case the precious files perched on the shelving rack would be deemed too hot a property to be overlooked by burglars, or in case the computer and its load of top secret information would wet their appetite.

After he had shown her the injunction, the stammering solicitor rang up the relevant office to enquire about the case. It took her less than five minutes to get the lowdown, then she went on explaining to Idriz that the complaint had been lodged by none other than Mrs. Jones, and that the Environmental Health Officer had the power, if the problem persisted, to seize the noise-making equipment – at once the sole thought of losing his Yamaha gave him a sharp twinge in his chest.

Mrs. Jones lived just across the road from them. Her late husband used to place a few, cautious bets in the same agency Idriz and Artan had chosen as their own playground, when he was still alive. His demise had been as sudden as unexpected. Nowadays Mrs. Jones was seen stumbling forth, up and down the road, on her rickety crutches, limping from home to the GP for the weekly assessments, or, in the best case scenario, stretching as far as the supermarket, where she bought things small and light enough to be carried on her elbow. The orange, recyclable plastic bags were seen dangling from the grips of her sticks as she crawled back home. She was as blind and defenseless as she was nosy, her frailty hadn't diminished in the least her receptive faculties, and even though she could be said to have already one foot in the grave, she didn't miss a chance to eavesdrop on everyone falling into a radius of ten metres from her staggering frame.

'Ke-ke-keep th-the no-oise do-down,' stuttered the lawyer, 'a-and there wo-wo-won't be anymo-more pro-pro-problems.'

'The best advice I've ever been given is: you can do it. The best advice I can give to anyone is: if it is to be, it's up to me,' twanged Sabrina Ronson from down under, stately enthroned at her desk, in the video message aimed at all jobless people who might happen to tune in on her very own channel of hope. Her matronly presence was topped by smooth waves of noticeably dyed, honey-blonde hair, the robust contour of her torso was exalted by the grey, pinstriped blazer she wore, and by a midriff band of white lace embroideries. An eye-catching white buttonhole rose in full bloom added even more refinement to her queenly figure. A cascade of almond-sized pearls dangled from her neck and two more, cherry-sized pearls swung from her earlobes as she lectured.

'I was just a legal secretary,' she disclosed, 'and sometimes I wonder, how did I get where I am?' Her hands drawing circles as she evangelised.

Owing to the circumstance that the course only ran from Monday to Thursday – Fridays being reserved to the induction of a new batch of aspirants – when Lady Davina invited Ritchie, on Thursday evening, to keep her entertained with his truly enjoyable company, he replied he didn't have any objection to spending the afternoon of the following day engaging in pleasurable pastimes.

'I have two tickets for a movie, at the Oxo Tower,' she said enthusiastically.

'Sounds good,' he butted in.

'There is a Bollywood themed festival on. Do you like Indian cinema?'

'Sure, it should be interesting,' he commented. 'Buddhism has contributed to enlarge my views on the Asian continent of late. I am often reading about India or the Far East.'

'How about Indian food? Do you like it?'

'Yes, I do. I like chicken korma, and tikka masala... I have tried some of the most popular curries, although if they are too spicy I might have a reaction.'

'Uhm, what kind of reaction, exactly?'

'Well, it's a bit embarrassing... I... Start sweating. But in rather unusual places.'

'Like where?'

'At the nape, over the eyebrows, my face gets flushed and hot, drops of sweat trickle gently down into my shirt collar. It can be awkward.'

'I see, I was led to imagine steamier reactions,' she insinuated.

'They do say spices increase stamina, don't they?'

'Maybe,' she murmured, giggling.

This time there were no hitches. Ritchie turned up even a couple of minutes earlier. They met under the red-brick portico, by the riverside, at the foot of the Oxo Tower. He clocked in in his faded grey denims, black leather shoes – on the authenticity of the leather he had nurtured doubts from day one, as soon as he had ogled the boots, on their pyramidal stand, in the shop down Portobello Road – white shirt and black blazer. A smart casual combo. Lady Davina sagged in a wicker chair, by the coffee shop that she had decreed should be their meeting nest, she was perusing a leaflet – the festival calendar in all likelihood. She stood to greet him.

'How was your journey?'

'Quite smooth,' he said, stooping a little to kiss her on both cheeks.

'What are you having?' she asked.

Ritchie sat down with his back to the shop window. From there he could take in, at a glance, the promenade, the river and the river banks. The usual easterly winds had been funnelled into the Thames estuary and were running amok now, impressing on the silvery water a menacing series of indentations. The sky was just as leaden and dull in colour, except for patches of lighter grey fraying into pure white in the distance.

'Green tea?' He threw in.

'Sure,' she said, and gesturing to a girl in black idling about ordered: 'could we have a cup of black coffee and a green tea please?'

The girl nodded and was instantly sucked past the glass doors, as if the wind itself had blown her in. Luckily, the nook where they were safely parked was partially screened by the side wall and the pillars, it would take a proper storm to dislodge them.

'I was seeing someone more or less your age before we met,' said Lady Davina when the two china cups and their saucers had landed. 'It was going quite well, then all of a sudden he seemed to have scruples, recriminations... All sorts of issues about the two of us being involved at a deeper level began to crop up. He said I was too much of a mother figure for him to handle well, and that the last thing he wanted was to be cuddled and stroked by mummy. It felt unnatural somehow, odd, those were his words.'

'A consistent age gap between lovers can be a problem sometimes,' Ritchie philosophised, 'especially when the she in question is much older than he is. What happens is, everything the younger of the two says or does can be easily misinterpreted. The susceptibility of a mature lady can play strange tricks on her mind. In my opinion, she might resent things being said to her even when there was no real intention to hurt or offend.' He dipped his upper lip into the hot brew and took a small sip of green tea, but the tip of his tongue was badly scorched. His cup was duly returned to the saucer.

Around noon she suggested it was perchance time to have lunch, before going to the movies. He wasn't particularly keen on the prospect of stuffing himself with food rich in calories and then flop on a cushioned seat in the dark, it wasn't exactly his idea of fun. However, upsetting Lady Davina's plans for the day was the last thing he wanted. He guessed he might get away with snoozing his way through the film undetected, or even resort to texting one or two of his online correspondents to kill the time.

She led him past the narrow and breezy passageway giving on to the back of the building, a gold-and-green paisley shawl elegantly draped around her shoulders. A dingy alley ran between the Oxo Tower and the Bargehouse, where the buffet and the show were to be attended. The Bargehouse had formerly been a warehouse, and it had a somewhat rundown look, beneath the glitz and glamour of the banners and posters broadcasting the glories of the festival.

In a pillared hallway – the pillars were peeling and so was the ceiling – over a long row of tables clothed in red, trays, plates and bowls with all sorts of eastern dishes had been colourfully arranged.

'Fancy a samosa?' said Lady Davina, snatching one of the puffy triangles from a heap in a white ceramic dish and dipping it in a pot of mint sauce.

'Is it hot?' Ritchie said, staring goggle-eyed at her as if he was expecting something dreadful to happen.

'Yum, well, the filling is hot, but not particularly piquant. I gather it's rather mild.'

'Okay, I am gonna have to trust you,' he said, picking his own triangle from those lying near the base of the pyramid, since they were supposed to be cooler than the ones on top. This must be the moment of truth for him. He bit a corner of pastry, tossed it nervously about on his tongue, chewed it, and swallowed it. No danger of fires so far, his facial skin was not flushed, no rashes appeared on it, and no traces of sudor moistened it. Setting aside his fears, he finished the yummy appetiser and followed her onward to the next stage of the buffet. They had a couple of falafels each, and moved on to the main courses, where shredded chicken fillets were drowned in smoking hot, yellow and orange dips, next to mountains of rice and pools of brown curry, forests of fried vegetables and hillocks of glazed chick peas.

She kept scooping up helpings into a paper plate held in her left hand, and from there craning the food into her mouth with fluent action and undaunted grace of movement. He was a tad more rigid and stand-offish, but only through having to dodge the fieriest ingredients, lest his head catch fire like the tip of a match.

Buffet done and dusted, they headed for the theatre. The film was about to start. There was a minute or two of indecision regarding where to seat, the choice being of far deeper consequences than a simple selection of the best visual angle entailed, according to the latest studies in fact the inner cogwheels of a person's psychology could be revealed by the position assumed in front of the big screen. Those who occupied central seats were said to be confident, decisive, assertive personalities, whereas those heading for the back seats, but still aiming for a full-frontal experience of the show, were deemed to be calm and collected individuals, even though, opting to stand significantly back from the action, they might be considered somehow timid and afraid of others' influence, to a degree. Those who settled down in the middle rows – the study went on explaining – with the screen looming off-centre, might be said to crave personal space and be exclusively attracted to people they feel an affinity with. Cornering yourself up right at the back might be the sign that you want to have a global view of what's going on but struggle to get involved on a personal level, detachment being a clear index of lack of confidence, unless of course you feel inclined toward anonymity for tactical reasons, such as the impelling need of smooching your lady friend, for instance.

Needless to say, Ritchie and Lady Davina, after the above-mentioned brief moments of substantial teetering, beelined all the way to the back rows, squeezing themselves between the fourth and third to last row of padded chairs, rather centrally.

Even more Indian food popped up on the screen soon after the movie opening credits. In a cramped kitchen a pensive housewife juggled saucepans and oil jars, sifted breadcrumbs, chopped aubergines, rolled up sweet balls, deep fried and sautéed with sapient wrist and elbow swift jerking motion, the steam wafting above the stove painting a veil of moisture on her focused expression.

'Did you enjoy the buffet?' whispered Lady Davina, transfixed by the housewife's cooking manoeuvres.

'Of course,' Ritchie said, 'the food was above average.'

'I wish I could have won my husband's affection through cooking him titbits, too!' she added.

As a matter of fact, that's what the housewife was trying to accomplish, she wanted to prepare her husband such delicious delicacies for lunch that would have put some fire back in their relationship. Once the food was ready, she poured it into metallic pots, into separate containers that could be piled up into a cylindrical canister. She slipped the canister into a pistachio-green jute bag and took it downstairs, in the courtyard, where she went on tying it to a stand loaded with several other lunchboxes. Here the delivery boy entered the scene, in white linen trousers and white baggy untucked shirt, white side cap, and thin black mustache. Surely he was past his prime for a delivery boy. The canisters were all hitched to his bike, one by one, to the handlebars, to the seatpost, to the parcel rack. Finally, he took to the pedals, and on he rode, beside menacing, long queues of vehicles, on the roads of the bustling tropical metropolis, to hand out to indefatigable employees their well-deserved home-made meals.

At this point Lady Davina casually outstretched her right arm across the back of Ritchie's seat, then her hand was launched into a tentative exploration of his right shoulder, climbing all the way up, like a crawling spider, creeping up to his nape and alighting there, the palm landing outspread at the base of his neck. He looked at her inquisitively.

'I am just making sure you are not having a reaction,' she assured him.

His mature flame seemed to be friskier than usual today, more adventurous than on their previous rendezvous. Maybe even a bit too forward for his liking.

Now her hand came down, and another ascent began, in the region of his left thigh.

Meanwhile, the lunch lovingly made by the housewife had been taken round to the wrong address, to a senior accountant into a buzzing office, rather than to her husband. The biker boy had swapped it with the takeaway the accountant had been used to order from a nearby restaurant. Anyhow, the fellow didn't seem to be excessively displeased with the contents of the food canister brought to his desk, he ate with gusto, forgetful of stacks of papers and esteemed colleagues fading in the background.

'I see where this is going,' Lady Davina observed, 'yet another case of romance between blooming youth and grey old age.'

'He isn't grey,' Ritchie cut in, 'his hair is still pretty much black, so is the mustache.'

'He is about to retire though, and that means he must be past sixty or thereabouts, unless in India they retire in their fifties, which would be comforting, encouraging somehow.'

'It might not be love either, let's wait and see. They might never get to meet each other after all,' he sneered.

As it happens the housewife and the old accountant, thrown together by mere accident, were having an epistolary conversation. He had had the brilliant idea to write a note, evaluating the dishes brought to his attention. She had come to realise it wasn't to her husband her culinary creations were being sent, but the novelty had sparked enough curiosity to elicit a response from her, as a result the correspondence was on, it was engrossing the audience.

'And yet it is so romantic, don't you find?' Lady Davina said. Inadvertently her voice had been raised a few bars, a few too many for those sitting within earshot. A sibilant 'shush!' was suddenly fired at them from somewhere nearby, an unidentifiable source. And another, and yet another one, coming from such disparate directions they seemed to emulate the stereophonic effect of the surround sound.

Confirming Ritchie's bleak forecast, the accountant and the housewife never got to meet, although they had been planning to do so. Their moving story ended rather bitterly, or else, it lacked a well-defined ending. Their written acquaintance never really moved on to the next stage. When the final credits rolled, Ritchie heaved a sigh of relief, two hours in the musty darkness, divided between the heartrending storyline and Lady Davina's rambling advances, had thoroughly done his head in. Plus he felt bloated, his stomach was awkwardly swelling and worryingly hyperactive. He needed to retire, to unwind, to break wind, to let gaseous clouds out of his rumbling tummy.

'I truly enjoyed it,' he said, beaming from ear to ear.

'I'll be flying out to Canada in two days' time,' she pleaded.

Ritchie didn't budge. This time around he was in no mood to take her home, there would soon be some other occasion.

Having spent most of the night flatulating freely – when he had shared the bed with Lady Davina he had had to hold on to his vapours almost to the point that it had felt unbearable, unnatural, trying to release turbulences without external vibrations had been a wearisome task – and part of the morning appeasing his digestive system, sprinkling it with reinvigorating fruit juices and feeding it delicate jam tarts, to recover from the Indian binge, he readied himself to look in on Artan, at the office, in what promised to be an eventful afternoon at the races. At three fifty the Ascot Chase was due to raise the roof, and give their winning hopes a clamorous boost, or maybe a sound thrashing, who knows, but morale was high. This was the day they were going to get back on their feet, if not conclusively at least in terms of pride, Ritchie had no doubts, and Artan had faith in him, in the Buddha's infallible divinatory sense.

They both had set eyes on a dapple grey thoroughbred, seven-year-old Bolder, who twelve months earlier, right here, on the prestigious stage of this beloved track, had come second, beaten only by a hair's breath, in a twist of fate of catastrophic proportions, rather than for his own fault. Bolder was faultless, and flawless, a beauty to watch galloping on the greenest turf you could ever find in the land. Today though there would be no last minute heartaches, the champion horse was in for a blazing victory.

The betting shop was packed. Idriz and his clan were there, Dritan, Sokol, Liridon, Edonis, Isuf and Saban, all looking in good spirits. In the fruit machines corner Uncle Tariq and Grandpa Andri held council, striking the poses of an old couple of lords having a tea break during routinely parliamentary labours. Their faces were grave, either for the solemnity of the moment or just because they had been forced out of the house at ungodly hours by the children's early stirring. The Chinaman was there, too. After the recent debacle he had resorted to prayer, a beaded rosary of eastern making was coiled around his wrist – it might be amethyst, or a cheap imitation of the semi-precious stone – and a bright yellow tassel tickled the palm of his hand and his fidgety fingers. His head also seemed to sway gently back and forth, as if he were working his magic to cast evil spirits away, and bring good luck on himself. The Qasooris were there, confabulating in a close circle, and keeping to themselves as always – the family was their whole universe. They were dressed to impress, and could easily pass for a local gang of mustachioed Mafiosi. The Farells on the other hand – distinguished butchers of wide renown – cracked quips lightheartedly, in a flush of pink faces and rubicund, puffy cheeks.

Ritchie and Artan had decided to join forces, perhaps standing united against rotten luck would be beneficial, or so they had devised, therefore they staked fifty quid each in a straight bet of a ton on Bolder to win, four to one Bolder.

'We're in for a win, mate!' exulted Ritchie.

Artan gave him a buoyant, trusting smile, and side by side they stood expectantly in front of the screens to face the final verdict, a reassessment of their karma.

They were off. Suspense and trepidation took over, all eyes were riveted to the screens, and a sepulchral silence descended on the room and the gamblers, levelling all social disparities. Idriz and his clan were the first to break the spell, they took to root noisily for their favourite, Petit Moi. The Chinaman swayed his head more vehemently now, muttering incomprehensible, half-chewed words, which sounded pretty much like: 'om-mam mani-mam, om-mam mani-mam, om-mam...' His new song had none of his previous, anglicised incitements, in it. Most probably he rooted for Ma Morgause. The Qasooris groaned, and their jaws dropped. The Farells followed the horses' evolution on the turf with their arms folded, a stance they had not much chance to practise when hurrying about in the shop. Ritchie and Artan endured the most harrowing interlude of their entire lives. All it took was five crosses between English mares and Arab stallions and five minutes hurtling on a stretch of grass to redefine their beliefs, the past, the present, the future, the planet, their place in the cosmos, life and death... All the cards were being reshuffled under a heavy stomping of hooves.

To be entirely honest, the only little blemish, in an otherwise perfect racing horse, was Bolder's uneasiness when confronting fences. On more than one occasion he had unseated his jockey, but that phase was over now, he was more mature at fences, and the way he sailed forth, jumping magnificently, was the incontrovertible proof of it. On Bolder flew, pressing the leader, Petit Moi, while Ma Morgause closed up threateningly, having bypassed Ballistic and Theatre Goer. Ritchie and Artan were already visualising four hundred feverish pounds in crisp notes of twenties – the odd fifty-pound note thrown in for good measure – when the unimaginable came into being. At the last fence Bolder ducked from left to right and Walsh, the jockey, was flung from the saddle and hurled violently over the fence, landing on his back. Ma Morgause rode on to victory, followed by Petit Moi. Yet another beautiful dream had been cruelly shattered.

'Ma-Ma Morgoose, Ma-Ma Morgoose,' yelped the Chinaman, tears welling up in his eyes.

'You funked it, stupid mare!' Ritchie wept, ripping up his ticket.

Later in the evening he burnt more candles on his private altar of healing and redemption. He wished he could be miles away from all the grief and misfortune that hovered around him, and that gathered over him like a negative halo he'd rather swap with a luminous, and saintly one. How joyous it would have been to experience the simple life of a Tibetan monk in the rarefied air of Himalayan plains, to embrace a return to nature and to basic pleasures. To welcome the rigours of winter as a salubrious backdrop and to take in the sight of the icy crests and of the whole immense amphitheatre where the scene of his purification would be salvifically enacted. That would have been pure bliss.

'The ground sprinkled with perfume and spread with flowers,' he recited, 'the Great Mountain, four lands, sun and moon, seen as a Buddha Land and offered thus, may all beings enjoy such Pure Lands. I offer without any sense of loss the objects that give rise to my attachment, hatred, and confusion, my friends, enemies, and strangers, our bodies and enjoyments; please accept these and bless me to be released directly from the three poisons.'

Then he chanted: 'IDAM GURU RATNA MANDALAKAM NIRYATAYAMI.' And a deep sense of peace descended on him and inhabited his crouching body. His enhanced perception felt like a glowing carbuncle at the centre of his body, this was the hub around which his whole, new life, irradiated with renewed energy.

In 1936, after a series of inspiring visions, Dada Lekhraj, a respected and wealthy member of a spiritual community based in Hyderabad, had consistently expanded his own, and his disciples' knowledge about the nature of the soul, of God, and of that puzzling enigma that is time. Sharing his visions, he awakened the whole community's awareness of those essential concepts – essential an in: of vital importance for anyone willing to live a spiritual, and meaningful life. On the strength of such revolutionary revelations the Brahma Kumaris study centre had been resting its foundations, like a phoenix reborn from the ashes of the old guru. Today the group's meditation centres were successfully attended by thousands of students worldwide.

In a compact building topped by a white frieze, and adorned with a sun-shaped high window, the Brahma Kumaris World Spiritual University provided enduring enlightenment for all those seeking peace, truth, and communion with the supreme being, only a five-minute walk away from Ritchie's humble abode.

On a nippy and grey Sunday afternoon, squatting on the lustrous parquet of the gym-sized hall, people from all walks of life were meditating on the perks of meditation.

'The most important journey you can take,' reiterated their Indian guru, a goateed guy with curly, unkempt hair

71

and rectangular specs in a white T-shirt bearing the university's logo, 'is the journey within, the final destination of this journey is an amazing discovery, the discovery of the truth of who you really are. Meditation alone enables you to undertake this inward journey, and gives you the necessary tools for it. Raja Yoga meditation, especially, helps you gain a clear spiritual understanding of yourselves, working toward the building of your character, and contributing to develop new strengths and qualities, together with a new, positive attitude to life.' The guru paused, shut his eyes and placed his hands, palms up, on his bent knees. Then he inhaled slowly and solemnly. 'Please repeat the exercise after me,' he said, and the room heaved a collective, soul-filling sigh. 'Meditation, accurately directed, makes God accessible to everyone,' he went on, his eyelids trembling as if he were just about to levitate off the parquet. He remained firmly anchored, though.

In the sixth row of crouching students, fourth from the end of the row nearest the door, breathed in Jess, still as a marble. Not even her filigree earrings – turquoise teardrops framed by intricate wirework of oxidised silver – were flinching. The trick must be working after all; she must be on her way to find herself.

At twenty past six, on the Station Parade, Ritchie paced nervously the pavement. He, too, was breathing, exhaling plumes of hot breath while staring at the station clock. She was running late.

'I am sorry, but my phone is dead and I couldn't call you to tell you I was going to be a bit late,' Jess apologised as soon as she arrived.

'No worries!' he said. 'Better late than never.'

'I thought you were going to be taller,' she observed.

'I see. I am sorry to disappoint you.'

'Don't get me wrong, you are quite tall, only, I imagined you would be taller, that's all.'

They dawdled down the high road in the deepening darkness of the evening. When they had walked halfway through the high road he pointed at the residential area where he lived.

'I live at the end of this road,' he mumbled, but she deliberately ignored his invitation.

'I live not far from here as well,' she said, 'maybe ten or fifteen minutes away, around Queen's Park station.'

Once they had marched all the way down to the bus garage and back again, he proposed a celebratory drink in the pub on Walm Lane. The Kingsbury was nothing but a mock-Tudor house that had converted into a posh boozer. On a flat screen mounted in a corner a trite sitcom, muted and subtitled, was on, when Ritchie and Jess entered the lounge. A group of boys and girls were chilling out on the chesterfield, in front of the fireplace. Ritchie and Jess settled down on a padded bench, at the twelve-foot rustic table.

'I want to go on a six-month tour of South America,' she jabbered, 'backpacking, and exploring the continent.'

'Why, aren't you happy with how things are going?'

'My job is stressing me out. I have to look after unruly nippers from Monday to Friday, and then babysit at the weekend... I have no time for myself, and I am not getting any younger either.'

'Okay, but South America sounds a bit too extreme.' he objected.

'I need something to shake me up, something different, a challenge.'

'Join the army!' he quipped.

Her earrings were flinching now. They rocked while she shifted her gaze from her sweaty glass to his reddening face. When their toe-dipping chat was over he walked her to Queen's Park. She had to resort to a short speech on the health benefits of vigorous strolls along tree-lined avenues, to persuade him to get that far from his block, on an evening that promised to get drizzlier and much cooler.

'Do I get a kiss now?' he threw in when they were about to part.

'Don't be silly,' she shrilled. 'I never kiss anybody on the first date.'

'That's sad. How about on the second date?'

'Not even on the second,' she said. 'I am looking for my soulmate.'

Mr. Idriz and associates were busy soundproofing the family's retreat that night.

'With these on the walls you can play as much as you like!' Howled Edonis, carrying a polystyrene sheet into the incriminated living room.

'I am gonna throw the biggest party this neighbourhood has ever seen!' Idriz vowed, steadying himself on the stepladder.

'Old lady crazy woman, you don't mind her!' Spluttered Uncle Tariq, a puff of smoke whiffing out of his wispy mustache.

The children were rolling about on the carpet strewn with tiny white pellets of polymer, taking advantage of the synthetic blizzard to romp and caper with a vengeance.

'Old lady soon will die!' Prophesied Uncle Tariq. 'She falls face down, and croaks, like a mangy dog!'

Idriz was almost thrown off balance by the convulsive laughter that gripped his guts. Edonis doubled up with laughter as well, and Grandpa Andri and Adelina chuckled a few feet away.

'Then we go on the grave, at night,' Uncle Tariq dug in, 'and piss on her. We do big party, I buy the drinks!'

Lying supine and rigid in bed, Ritchie struggled to fall asleep that night. All kinds of visions were crowding his mind. They were not quite the visions of Dada Lekhraj, or those of the other holy men of India, oh, no, he wasn't anywhere near the spiritual emancipation of his revered masters. His life had come to be an impenetrable muddle, and an unsolved enigma. Plus he was finding increasingly harder to get what he wanted from the girls, or from people in general. Maybe his magic touch was wearing out, and his savoir fare and his charisma were coming to an end. His best qualities were being brutally stifled by the harsh reality that had seeped into the fortress of his faith. On top of that money seemed to be perennially on the way out, and the red figures in his bank balance outdid by a worryingly wide margin the green ones. The traffic light of his wealth had stalled and was stuck on the no go. There was no flow, and no outlet for his dreams and aspirations. He was bottled up in the grey limbo of eternal return. He was the stray dog that bites his tail. His soul couldn't get past the weight of the world and float into pure dharmadhatu.

Week two of the Job Access was more or less plain sailing. Once it had been clear that, no matter what, job or no job, nobody would have been kicked out of the welfare bandwagon, little anxieties and initial awkward sparks of misgiving gave way to gentler sets of feelings and to meeker tempers. A stocky chap, whose black long hair was tied in a braid at the back, and whose hairy arms bore tattooed inscriptions that required much decoding, kept turning up at least one hour later than nine. He stormed in panting, apologising in a lilt that was one third proletarian, one third cockney and one third Anglo-Asian.

'Sorry Miss,' he'd tell Gloria, humbling himself like a fumbling schoolboy, 'there were problems with trains.'

'Okay,' she boomed. 'Take a seat.'

Despite his genuine acts of contrition though, he'd punctually arrive even later the day after, nibbling away from the total toll of course hours a few precious minutes here and there, or, in other words, parroting the mean cunning practised by employers when handling their staff, and the sly tactics the government too applied in the management of its citizens' lives. He was not going to have any of that, as his tattoos warned. 'Mess out with me, and I'll do the same to you,' would eventually be his unquestionable motto.

Even Jason's cockney twang, like the braided colossus's, sounded phoney after a while, and slightly contrived, and he admitted at last, during a friendly chat across desks with John the builder – Gloria had called a timeout – that his family as well had been hailing, some generations back, from the green pastures of Ireland, and only relatively recently had settled in London, on cockney land.

'As you can see from my accent,' he added.

John confirmed that family names such as Jason's were extremely popular in the county where he was from.

Gloria invited the class to wear formal attire for the last few days of the course.

'I am going to take photos of you. They will have to be stapled in your last book, and filed away,' she pointed out.

Some guys took the piece of advice quite literally, and twenty-four hours later could be seen pushing pens at their desks in black suit and silky tie combos that made them look like bankers rather than struggling unemployed. Ritchie took no heed of Gloria's advice, and kept wearing grey denims and grey sweater over a white shirt to the very end of the course. No point in sprucing up for Sabrina Ronson's archives, as far as he was concerned. John, too, kept coming in with his moss-green fleece prudently zipped all the way up, either because the lure of a suited career didn't appeal to him or else for paucity of wardrobe.

'If you dress to impress at a job interview, and look smart, and neat, like Ayo for example,' said Gloria, having given the fellow Nigerian an appreciative once-over, 'chances are you are already half way there.'

Ayo smirked smugly, and dived into his paperwork with renewed zeal.

'But if you dress like John,' she felt the need to add, 'no offence, John, I am only making my point; well, if you dress like John chances are you won't come across as someone keen, and presentable, whom they might want to hire,' she concluded.

John simpered amiably in the face of his alleged slovenliness. Probably what he cared most about was being clearly identified as an Irish man, rather than looking fit for work. He had actually begun to wear a gold cross stud earring, to give his laid-back look a final uninhibited touch. The guy must have relished the flamboyant style of the eighties, and that tiny cross pinned to his earlobe was a blatant manifesto of his penchant for it.

On Tuesday, right after midday break, Gloria set a new task for the class.

'You will go out in groups,' she dictated, 'and conduct a brief survey. You will have to pretend that you are mystery shoppers, and make sure that the premises you inspect are run smoothly and efficiently. I will give you a checklist, you will enter a shop of your choice, and check whether everything is being done according to health and safety rules and regulations, and if the place is customer-friendly.'

An unsettled murmur grew louder in the audience while these directions were given.

'What shop should we choose?' Asked Da Silva. Da Silva's command of the English language was barely sufficient, and he had, as a consequence, to speak at least twice every time he raised an objection. He wore rectangular onyx glasses and his skin colour wasn't easily identifiable. In his own words his most comprehensive work experience had been a stint into a big supermarket chain, where he had been wheeling around and lifting crates of fruit and vegetables for most of his shifts.

'Any shop you like,' cackled Gloria. 'But make sure you spread out. Each group must go into a different shop. Understood?'

'Yeah,' an Indian chap agreed. He wore photochromic lenses, with the result that when sunlight, breaking through the clouds, beamed into the classroom, his dark shades gave him a lugubrious appearance. He would often ramble on, even though nobody interjected or sparred with him in verbal contentions. He'd start firing an opinion, or cracking a joke, and then go on and on, unprovoked, until exhaustion overcame him.

Jason, Ali and Ritchie ended up being dispatched together on the delicate mission. After much deliberation they headed for a large sportswear store. They dropped nonchalantly in and took to survey the place, or rather to check out cool trainers and tees, ticking the relevant boxes on their checklists.

'This is just a waste of time!' said Jason downcastly.

'Yeah, I am not going to approach the staff to ask them questions,' Ali agreed.

'We don't need to,' Ritchie chipped in. 'Let's just fill the form here, quietly,' he went on, sitting on one of the comfy blue puffs in the shoes department. 'Then we'll go back.'

When the task was over they scattered out in a huff. It was blustery on the Olympic Way. Dark, menacing clouds stretched to the horizon, travelling fast on the impetuous gusts. There they were, three out-of-work idlers, three good-for-nothings, while all around them the city strived to be productive, and office workers milled about in dark suits, and secretaries trotted firmly on in their winter coats, and coffees were avidly slurped on the go through paper cup lids, and cigarettes were nervously and furtively smoked, in corners and recesses, before getting back into the workplace to be of service. Whereas they reeled like three little lost lambs out there, in the wide, bare avenue. They felt misplaced, and hurried back without further ado to number one, and to room four, up on the twelfth floor, to rejoin their comrades-in-arms.

Two days before the course came to a conclusion the turbaned girl landed a job. She had thoroughly enjoyed her McDonald's fatty lunches, but eventually the fear of uncertainty, and of a bleak future on the dole, had played a major part in defeating her impressionable soul. She wasn't as callous as the older guys. In fact, they couldn't give a toss if the future looked bleak, since they were determined to look bleaker. No job meant to them a lot more time in bed, in the morning, and at the pub in the evening. To Ritchie it meant a lot more focus on his spiritual progress, and some extra time for the girls, of course. Surely, he would have had time for them even after work, but can you actually compare going out at the end of eight stressful hours in a hostile environment, with doing it after a few hours of essential meditation and liberating spiritual practices? Going out after work would imply carrying with you a load of additional anxieties that did nothing to improve your performances with the damsels. Oh, no, a job would turn out to be useful only as a business card filler, when you had to introduce yourself. It gave you a title. 'What do you do for a living?' was what they'd generally ask you, and, 'I am...' followed by your job title, was what would proudly ensue, admitting you'd have a job to be proud of. But what if you hadn't? What if you were forced to say, in all truth, I am a shop assistant, a cleaner, a receptionist, a road sweeper, a dog walker? What would your date's reaction be to such ignominious announcements? A reaction that would make you cringe most probably. Therefore, it could almost be said that having no job was better than having one, in some very special circumstances. And Ritchie's circumstances were special indeed. He needed not abide by mass labels and unsubstantiated judgements, he could

80

do without all that. 'No, thank you!' was his adamant reply to such subtle manipulations.

'It is also very important that you smell nice, when going to a job interview,' Gloria lectured implacably. 'Some people have a bad odour, they aren't too keen on washing and on personal hygiene, and that doesn't make for a good first impression!'

A dreadlocked Rasta miss with red cat-eye glasses resented that.

'Why, it might be not their fault if they smell!' she cried.

'I am not saying it must necessarily be their fault, but turning up for an interview stinking like a homeless person is not the best introduction to a new job, that's all!' Gloria made clear.

'Poor them!' the Rasta miss blurted out. 'Not only they have a skin problem, because that's what it is, some people's skin is more pongy than others', on top of that they must also face blunt rejection!'

She looked like a prematurely aged old girl. Her slim figure and childish features stood out in neat contrast with the fantasy charity-shop cardigans and woolly trousers she used to wear, which hailed from two decades back and were fit for a pensioner. Indeed, that's what happened to these boys and girls after years out of work, they seemed to pull off a giant leap from adolescence to retirement, skipping the entire middle part of their lives, for instance the one that should be taken up by a career.

'I always try to smell nice!' yelled Da Silva from the back of the room. 'I shave every morning, I wash, and I put on some deodorant...' He groaned, while the crumpled tissues with which he was wiping his runny nose multiplied over his desk. He was sowing the pestiferous germs of influenza.

On the penultimate day of the programme two ladies popped in, late in the morning, to recruit volunteers. Gloria gladly let them take centre stage and preach to the unbelievers, for about ten to fifteen minutes, about the paramount importance of doing voluntary, unpaid work, in order to gain new skills and indispensable references.

'My colleague and I will distribute some leaflets with our address and telephone number,' said the leader of the duo, a brown-haired curly forty-something in casual attire – she wore a manly black bomber jacket. 'Just give us a call, and believe me, nothing will benefit you more than doing voluntary work right now. We were unemployed like you,' she let out, 'before we took on this offer, and now we have a job!'

The class was speechless.

'Are you going to call the voluntary work association then?' wondered Gloria at the next tea break.

'Mmm, yes, why not? I might do that!' Ritchie said, nodding emphatically. They were in the kitchenette.

'Is that water boiling hot?' she asked curtly, since he was pouring water from the kettle into his paper cup.

'Yes, it is.'

'Can you pour some into my mug, please?'

'Sure,' he said, filling her mug to the brim.

The final task of the course was mock interviews. The jobseekers were to form pairs, and to conduct a thorough assessment of each other's curriculum vitae. The pairs would have to be formed at random, choosing names scribbled on scraps of paper from a bowl. Jason picked up Ritchie's name.

'I don't have much to say, really,' Ritchie warned him.

'Okay, don't worry mate, I'll keep it short and sweet!' Jason said.

Ritchie was feeling slightly dizzy, and that must be very likely because the germs that Da Silva had been sneezing out were polluting the air. Da Silva's noxious spray was definitely having a debilitating effect on him, he realised, so much so that he went through the mock interviews exercise with his waterproof jacket thrown over him blanket fashion, and pulled up to his chin.

'You see, mate,' Jason said – it was his turn to be grilled – 'I am a qualified printer, and the reason why I am here is, I won't work for less than four hundred quid per week.'

'That makes sense,' Ritchie put in.

No sooner had the mock interviews ritual come to an end, than Gloria started to wrap up the course. The part-time receptionist who had intermittently been seen in the hall strutted sensuously in. She had a red tartan skirt on, and knee-high black stockings, and a hart and a rose were inked respectively on her right and left thigh. 'Yes Gloria,' she purred in a plummy, and sibilant voice, almost taking a light bow. Gloria whispered some instructions to her. A couple of minutes later the tattooed receptionist reappeared with a filing box, she laid the box on the floor, made her reverence once again, and off she tiptoed on her high-heeled stilettos. Gloria went about ordering the books of exercises in neat stacks held together with rubber bands, then she stowed them scrupulously away into the filing box. The remaining forty-five minutes were spent chit-chatting at ease. At last the class was granted leave and, with the hint of regret that always weighs down on someone's heart when something is irremediably about to end, the boys and girls dispersed out there, in the corridor. They regrouped in the hallway, by the lifts, and were shuttled down, to the ground floor, in two separate batches. Finally, the jobseekers were sieved past the revolving door and scattered out on the Olympic Way. Will they ever meet again? Who knows? Hardly, judging from the diffident glances they had been directing at each other during those momentous last instants of association.

'That's what happens when you are a team player,' Ritchie grumbled later on in the evening, in marked nasal tones. He was having his thousandth phone conversation with mum. 'You get the flu.'

'What did the poor chap have to do? It's not his fault if he was unwell,' Janet Barker said.

'Okay, mum, but you can't just go and spread a virus like that.'

'He should have worn a mask; I'll give you that.'

'Bloody Da Silva!' Ritchie cursed.

That night he had to sleep in the most uncomfortable position ever, minding to keep his nose straight up, and pointed at the ceiling, for the least inclination on either side meant mucus flooding his air passages and stifling him. A clogged nose would also have obliged him to breathe through the mouth, which was highly undesirable.

A famous episode of the life of Buddha suddenly came to mind. On one occasion Buddha had starved himself so thoroughly that he wasn't even able to stand up and go about his business as usual, and feebly stumbling forward, he had eventually lost his senses and plunged unconscious into a river. Hadn't been for a bunch of villagers rescuing him from the turbulence of the stream he'd have lost his life. It was exactly after these events that the Buddha had devised there should be a third, milder path leading to enlightenment, and that extreme measures and unnecessary mortifications had to be eschewed.

As soon as he was back on his feet Ritchie texted Sheila.

'Hey, what's up?'

'Nothing, as usual.'

'Wanna hang out?'

'What do you have?'

'French Shiraz.'

'Okay, when?'

'Tomorrow?'

Yup, tomorrow's fine!'

She breezed into Ritchie's flat carrying her laptop, in a professional-looking case, dug it out, opened it on the reclaimed teak coffee table and took to type briskly away.

'What are you doing?' wondered Ritchie.

'Some work. Do you mind?' she said without lifting her eyes from the screen.

'What sort of work is that?' he asked.

'It's for a company, The Greener Grass,' she went on. 'They make artificial green walls and install it all over England.'

'Smashing! And what is your role exactly?'

'Right now I have been assigned a tough task, I have to come up with a new slogan.'

'Wow! Have you tried: I see green?'

'Nah, too bold.'

'Where the grass is always greener?'

'Too obvious.'

As she scrolled the company's website, the various panels of synthetic grass on sale came up one by one. They looked like bouquets on tiles, ready to be slotted into a wider composition. The promotional blurbs introducing each panel were quite striking: Devon, a veil of luscious greens dotted with delicate flowers; Northumberland, a tumble of wild grasses and earthy ferns merged with claret-tinged foliage; Somerset, bringing together summer blossoms, grasses and delicate white flowers; Cumbria, an opulent display of verdant foliage enriched by claret-toned grasses; Kent, a manicured buxus widely recognised as an instant classic; Dorset, a collection of luscious plants composing a deluxe green patchwork; Suffolk, a feast of theatrical leaf forms pervaded by jewel tones of fuchsia and lively greens, Cheshire, a magical medley of deep greens with bursts of sprightly young leaves; Yorkshire, a dramatic backdrop of greens with a trail of fine cream blossoms; Cornwall, tufts of regal claret grasses interwoven with an explosion of greens; and last but not least Hampshire, a rich medley of foliage characterised by dramatic textures and tones. The wine list of the poshest West End restaurant couldn't have been more enticing. Even after a cursory glance at those squares of grass you felt compelled to buy and own them. Perhaps getting hold of a single panel would have been like having a unique piece of art to boast about and be proud of when friends would come around. It could have been just as well hung indoors, rather than out in the garden. According to The Greener Grass's eggheads and marketing gurus, their green walls had a therapeutic value, basically you stared at their bushes and your illnesses would go away.

'Look at our green walls, and you'll feel fine!' Ritchie blabbed on.

'Too long,' Sheila rebuked him.

'Greener Grass, the final cure to cancer!' he insisted, insensitively.

'You are the last person I should have gone to for advice, Ritch!' she lamented.

'Hey, I am just trying to be of help!'

'No, you are turning everything into a joke, which is all you ever do,' she said, folding the laptop and shoving it back into its case.

A mere four days later, she was back at his place.

'Do you know what happened when I left, last time?' she said.

'What happened?' Ritchie obliged.

'I met Tina, an old friend of mine, right here, at the bus stop.'

'Amazing! What did she say?'

'She said that if I wanted I could move in with her, in Hampstead, in a very large house she is the caretaker of.'

'Incredible!' he marvelled. 'So I guess your answer was yes.'

'It was,' Sheila said. 'And you know what?' she added.

'What?'

'The house she mentioned turned out to be the same one I was being employed at, a couple of years ago, as private nurse to the late Mrs. Dee, before I went to live with auntie.'

'What an uncanny coincidence!' Ritchie ejaculated.

'It was probably my mistake to leave the house altogether, two years ago, because you see, when Mrs. Dee passed away, her family told me I could stay if I liked, the house was going to be empty, and someone must be there to look after the place. So now Tina does the caretaking that was originally offered to me, and she said I could go and share the place with her. The house is empty and large, too large for one person not to feel cold and spooky.'

'What about auntie?' he probed.

'Well, you said I should ditch her didn't you?'

'I did indeed.'

'That's what I did.'

'Well done, congratulations!'

'Only, she didn't take it very well,' Sheila cut in timidly.

'What did she do?'

'She started saying I owed her money, one month rent at least, which amounts to about two hundred pounds, and until I won't give her the cash she will hold on to my clothes.'

'The old harridan is a proper bully!' Ritchie evinced. 'So you got no clothes now?'

'Just the few things I was able to carry with me in a small rucksack, the rest is in her wardrobe, locked away.'

In Sheila's opinion the late Mrs. Dee had been the kindest person on earth. She had taken her under her wing like a daughter, and in exchange Sheila had been as considerate and attentive of the old lady's needs as a real daughter should be, wheeling her around in those last few months, when she had been utterly unable to stand, feeding her lovingly, one spoonful at a time, and being careful not to spill any soup on her black crepe dress – she had been wearing black ever since her dear Malcom's gifted soul had been severed from his mortal spoils.

'Once her son, Michael, popped in at dinner time,' Sheila recalled, mildly amused, 'and told me off because I was spoon-feeding her prawns, which are non-kosher, although I didn't have a clue back then. I don't think that's appropriate, were his words. Please, do not give her any shellfish at all, he warmly recommended.'

'Yeah, it must have been daunting, having to watch out what to buy and what not for the old lady,' Ritchie surmised.

Back in 1969 Irene and Malcolm Dee had opened the doors of their north London Edwardian house to the young Jewish families of the neighbourhood. A weekly discussion group had thus been inaugurated, under the supervision of Rabbi Dr. Manzarek, and benefiting from the good auspices his oiled, pointy black beard and stern demeanour had instantly evoked upon the kinsfolk congregated for advice. The Jewish families had longed to be imbibed with the outstanding wisdom Dr. Manzarek's lecturing fury always oozed profusely. Irene had been a vaguely passé beauty in her late thirties back then, and Malcolm an accomplished director of The London Jewish Cultural Centre. He had successively become the chairman of the British Friends of the Hebrew University of Jerusalem, and later on in life, the director of the Friends of the London Jewish Cultural Centre limited. Their library was lined from floor to ceiling with bookcases laden with leather-bound volumes, and it was in this austere setting of oak panels, plush Persian carpets and fine upholstery that those eventful meetings had taken place. A strong sense of community had brought together the young Jewish families of the neighbourhood, and their sense of affiliation had never slackened, even when the young families had grown older, and the original tag coined for the group had come to sound a tad obsolete, or at least incongruous.

How time-worn and deserted the house looked now by comparison. An omnipresent stubborn film of dust had settled everywhere, giving the full measure of the futility of resistance to the new that replaces all that is old, and of the grim inevitability of decay, and downfall, even in such blessed dwelling, where life had once been so thriving and abundant. The girls' presence on the premises hadn't been thought up as a compact against the further advancement of that film of dust though, no, they were not there to wipe surfaces, but only to ensure there would always be somebody within, to reset the alarm in case it went off, or to ring Michael if something unusual was spotted out there, in the front yard or in the garden.

'There's a tennis court at the back of the house, too,' Sheila spilled out, 'and d'you know whom have I seen scampering about in shorts and trainers?'

'Whom?' Ritchie said.

'Gerry Goldwell. She seems to know the Dees quite well, actually she is a close neighbour. She lives just around the block.'

'Uhm,' Ritchie mulled over, 'strange that, with all the money she must have, she has to sneak into her neighbours' tennis court, and hasn't got one of her own.'

Geraldine Ester Goldwell, aged forty-two, was a singer-songwriter, an author, an actress, a fashion designer, a model, a television personality ginger bombshell, and God knows what else. She had come to prominence in the nineteen nineties as Ginger Space Girl, one of five members of the internationally acclaimed pop group, The Space Girls, which she left on the twenty-fifth of May 1998, on account of her increasing bouts of depression and widening differences with her colleagues. She had then gone on to embark on a dashing solo career, releasing hit singles at the speed of light, and bagging Brit Awards and platinum discs at an impressive rate. TV shows ratings had suddenly shot right up thanks to her bubbly personality and killer curves. Producers had fought hard to sign her on, they had drooled over her, and a new career had unexpectedly beckoned, making of her one of the best known British faces of all time. At one point she was deemed to be even more popular than some members of the royal family. The golden girl, or else a gold mine, that's what she had turned out to be, however, according to Sheila, she still had to rely on her neighbours' sports facilities.

'Don't you want to know whom she plays tennis with?' Sheila pressed on.

Ritchie rolled his eyes. He gave her another wary look, then said: 'whom?'

'Josh Michael!'

'No way! All the stars hang out at your place now.'

'He lives in the area, don't you know? You should read glossy magazines more often Ritch!'

Joshua Saul Papadopoulos, aged fifty-two, was yet another wonder of the pop world. He was an accomplished singer-songwriter and music producer, who from 1981 to present days had sold more records worldwide than the stars strewn over London's night sky, he had sold more than a hundred million records up until 2010. His bestselling album, Fame, had alone sold more than twenty million copies. He had been just as famous on home soil as abroad. At least eight of his number one hits had crept up on the Billboard Hot 100 in USA, plus he had won three Brit Awards, four MTV Video Music Awards, two Grammy Awards, three American Music Awards... He was super successful, acclaimed, and notoriously gay, despite the scores of young girls screaming and shouting at him every time he put in a public appearance, and despite the persistent pursuits of the more stubborn female fans, who on occasion had pushed their obsession with him beyond the boundaries imposed by the law and gone on to become stalkers by all means. Josh Michael had it all, and yet, in Sheila's words, he didn't disdain showing up, every now and then, on to his neighbours' backyard for a game of tennis with his old pal Goldwell.

'You should ask them an autograph,' Ritchie sneered, 'that's the least you ought to do!'

'Yeah, perhaps I will!'

Josh Michael had also been at the centre of some controversial episodes lately. One night he had been so high on weed he had crashed his car into a Snappy Snaps store, and one early morning he had been found slumped half-asleep at the wheel of a different vehicle on Hyde Park Corner, again in an extreme state of intoxication. At last he had candidly confessed his addiction, during a TV interview, rolling up one more funny cigarette right in front of the cameras, minutes before he was due to appear on stage, just to prove that the substance was innocuous. Needless to say, his reputation hadn't even been chipped by these testing ordeals. His public had loved him more, once his venial sin had been exposed.

Mrs. Dee's familiarity with Sheila and her genuine kindness stood out even more markedly now, in comparison to Tina's employer, yet another old Jewish lady, but much fiercer, and truly unpalatable.

'She shouts at her, either when they are alone or in public. She calls her names, and throws stuff at her, if Tina doesn't do at once what she says,' Sheila deplored.

'Nowadays things like that can be object of prosecution,' Ritchie suggested.

'How can she do that?' she mused. 'A Filipino girl with no connections, how can she square up to a well-known lady with family and friends. The lady is an influential person... She owns properties all over London and is highly regarded within the Jewish community.'

The rude old lady in question could often be seen traipsing down the road, between Mount Pleasant and Staverton Road. She grasped her duck-head walking cane with those claw-like hands of hers, and her corvine, dyed bob of hair was visible from a hundred yards away, owing to its fluffiness and quite impressive circumference. If anyone dared stand in her way, she'd petrify the unfortunate passer-by with one of her Medusa's flame-eyed stares. The neighbourhood, the city, the world was her oyster, or maybe her very own home ground, and there would be no mercy for trespassers.

After the fourth glass of excellent Shiraz, and all that talk about Hebrews and celebrities, or Hebrew celebrities, Ritchie thought wise to revert to business, the kind of business he was most keen on, tittle-tattle being surely not one of his strengths. His bare legs and feet were stretched out across the gorge that separated his bumblebee-yellow sofa from his reclaimed teak coffee table, like some kind of hairy drawbridge.

'So if you'll start hanging out with celebrities I won't be seeing you as often as of late, I suppose,' he threw in.

'They don't even know I exist, Ritch! I am like a garden gnome to them, or a slug. If they are really careful I might just not be kicked down or crushed underfoot when they are about,' she said, her words half-muffled by the violet-red contents of her inclined wine glass.

'Will we still be best buddies, then?' he insisted, taking in the curious sight of Sheila focusing on her drink, her pinkie unmannerly raised.

'We will!' she mouthed into the wine.

'Can you suck my cock now?' He hissed.

Ritchie was due to report at Kilburn jobcentre on the second Monday after the completion of Sabrina Ronson's eye-opening course. It was an overcast, and grey Monday morning, but dry, and not too cold either. Monday mornings were to him a cumbersome cross to bear, they were a burden. To everyone else they were the glorious beginning of a spanking new working week, to him they inevitably were all black Mondays, and he'd have scrapped them from the calendar altogether, unless they happened to be bank holidays – in which case of course they'd easily be smuggled up as Sundays.

Mondays had the sour aftertaste of a false start, and of unkept promises. They oozed with the rank smell of failure. However, as they were made, thankfully, and like any other day of the week, of twenty-four hours only, they'd eventually come to a close and expire, and together with them his guilty feelings and unuttered recriminations would be extinguished also. From Tuesday on, his week assumed a whole new meaning.

When he yanked open the first floor door and let himself into the stale office, girthy Williamson was conferring with another customer. Slouching on his desk, the exuberant adviser was preaching about the endless possibilities the jobcentre offered to those in need of aid. The blonde fifty-something unemployed lady sitting in front of him was nodding obediently and trying to coax Williamson into being as unselfish and informative as he could. Ritchie flopped on one of the badly stained sofas arranged in the centre of the room, where a lounging oasis had been created. The sofas were completely surrounded by the signing points. He had to choose his seat on the sofa very carefully, minding to avoid the greasier patches.

Twenty minutes later Williamson called out his name.

'Barker! Mr. Richard Barker!' he said, beckoning him over.

'Good morning,' Ritchie said, falling into the padded chair.

'How was the programme then?' Williamson inquired.

'It was very instructive,' Ritchie replied. 'It was hard work, too, we had to come up with quite a lot of answers, on a daily basis, but hopefully it will help improve chances of finding work.'

'It will indeed,' Williamson agreed, arching his eyebrows in a funny mask of complacency. 'And how did you get there, in the morning?' he then added.

'I took the Underground, the Job Access was only two stops away.'

'Have you kept receipts of your journeys?' the adviser rambled on.

'Sure,' said Ritchie, and produced a bundle of paper slips not at all dissimilar from those he used to get at the betting shop, with the difference that these ones related in detail the times and stops of his daily commute.

'Very well!' Williamson said, and took to lay the receipts down on his desktop like a hand of poker. Then he began scribbling sums at the foot of each receipt, once he had obtained the totals with the help of his calculator.

The operation lasted quite a while. It was interrupted, every now and then, by the ringing phone, and by the pointlessness of the inquiries the callers seemed to put forward. Plus girthy Williamson appeared to have no clue whatsoever as to the answers those inquiries should be given.

'I owe you thirty-three pounds and forty-five pence,' the adviser worked out. 'Is that correct?'

Ritchie looked puzzled, after all that fiddling with calculator pen and paper the chap was still asking if he was right. His question sounded a bit off, and rather preposterous. He got hold of his phone and quickly made up for Williamson's lack of accuracy, it took five seconds to establish how much his travels had cost him per day and then get the total over a two-week period.

'Yes, it should be right!' He confirmed at last.

Williamson headed for a door that needed unlocking. He dialled his pin code on the keypad, the door opened, and Williamson disappeared at the back. When he reappeared he had a form, and asked Ritchie to fill the form with his bank details so that he could be reimbursed.

'Can I see your card?' the adviser butted in.

Then, as Ritchie held it out, Williamson poked at the digits of the account number embossed on the card with the tip of his biro.

'These are the numbers you have to write down,' he explained.

Ritchie jotted down his account number, and the name of his bank, and when he had done, while Williamson processed the information, he lost a good five minutes scrubbing with the tip of his index finger the tiny ink mark left by Williamson's biro under his account number.

'All done,' the jobcentre employee said, 'you'll get paid today!'

'Thank you so much!' Ritchie rejoiced.

Many hours later, under cover of darkness, three shadowy silhouettes were seen skulking along in Balmoral Road. All three men were carrying what looked like a couple of petrol tanks each, from their handy, white Caddy van, parked somewhere down the row of terraced houses, in the only space available, to the Bosnia and Herzegovina Community Centre Advice.

'Let's give these beggars a wake up call, shan't we?' The chap leading the expedition, a skinhead fella in jeans and electric-blue jumper whispered.

'We shall indeed!' Chimed in one of his accomplices, a lanky guy with nerdy glasses and rotten teeth. Against his associates' advice the lanky guy had put on a brightly-coloured thing. In fact, he was wearing a white, long-sleeved top that was just a whit less conspicuous than a high visibility jacket.

The last bloke was the beefiest of the three, also the quietest. He only groaned, puffed and panted, or spoke in monosyllables, nodding and swaying his head as though he wasn't much concerned with the outcome of the blitz, or else as if he had grown so tired of words, that he had slowly but decidedly regressed to a primitive state. He looked tough, his nose was as flat as a boxer's nose, and his eyes were light blue, almost grey. He had been wise enough to wear darker clothes.

It must have been shortly after midnight when they broke in. The skinhead fella put down his two tanks of petrol, unhooked his crowbar from the carabiner clipped to his leather belt, like a gunslinger's weapon, and swiftly went on to force the main door of the Community Centre Advice.

'It's coming loose,' the toothless lanky guy spluttered, 'another little push, another little push...'

'Urgh!' Grumbled the skinhead, giving all he had in one last levering push, his shoulders and arms tensed for the exertion. Then the door gave in. It snapped open, and splinters flew all over from the entry point of the iron bar.

'Here you go, done!' Gloated the flat-nose guy.

In a jiffy they were in. The skinhead switched on the lights in the main hall, and in no time at all they sprinkled the place with gasoline.

'God if I love this fucking smell!' Roared the skinhead, 'it gives me a natural high.'

'Yeah, mate, even better than sniffing glue, isn't it? Joined in the toothless chap.

At twelve forty the fire brigade arrived at the scene, only six minutes after 999 had been dialled – fortunately, Willesden Fire Station was just around the corner. The call to the emergency service had been made by Mrs. O'Cannon. Mrs. O'Cannon taught at St. Andrew's primary school, and was very well known in the neighbourhood, because she was always fighting hard for the preservation of Gaelic customs, from St. Patrick's Day to the stobhach Gaelach. She had come out of her house in dressing gown and slippers, and seen the smoke on the roof of the Community Centre Advice, and had dialled 999 at once.

Rumours of the fire had circulated fast in the area, nevertheless Artan, Idriz and their clan only showed up at the crime scene the morning after, around seven. Uncle Tariq had given the alarm. He had been setting out on his daily collection round, and had spotted the investigators gathered outside the Community Centre Advice from the high road. The Kosovars were all standing on the other side of the road now, and looking on enraged.

'Arseholes!' Uncle Tariq yelled, juggling the fourth or fifth cigarette in the space of twenty minutes. 'These arseholes will pay. I take them with these hands,' he said, sticking the fag in his mouth and waving both hands, palms up, in front of him, 'and twist their neck, like chickens!' He promised, making the colourful gesture of clutching a neck with one hand and wringing it with the other.

Idriz looked a couple of shades darker than his usual dark. He just couldn't believe his eyes. The coppers were just hanging around and drawing conclusions in a relaxed fashion, as if judging the unharmful consequences of the fall of a few roof tiles, rather than focusing on avenging a serious act of racial hatred and of dire intolerance.

In the afternoon Ritchie dropped by, at the office. Not that he wanted to stretch out his losing record, he just strode in to see Artan, and have a friendly chat. As soon as the Kosovar relayed the night-time incident, though, his face froze in a mask of disgust.

'That's appalling, mate!' he condemned. 'I feel like I should apologise on behalf of the bloody nation for this act of senseless fanaticism.'

Artan coloured, his rosy skin tones were more rubicund and flushed than ever. It looked as if a map was traced in pink and red over his hollow cheeks.

'It is not our fault if your government accepted our application and gave us shelter, and a house, the doctor, and a school for our children. We are not breaking any law!' He maintained.

'The cowards who have done this are just a minority,' Ritchie comforted him. 'They are natural born losers, they are loonies, they have no principles, no shame, they could stab in the back their own friends and family members with the same cold brutality they showed in perpetrating this crime.'

Artan nodded vigorously, and blushed even more. Now the uncharted lands traced on his cheeks disappeared, for the skin was uniformly red.

'But as for the rest of us,' Ritchie went on, 'we have no issues whatsoever with you guys being here.'

'Thank you!' said Artan, and pulling out a folded copy of the *Racing Post* from his waist pocket pointed out that Vettori, the notorious, ever-winning Italian jockey, had failed yet another drug test in France and had therefore been banned for six months by the French racing authority. The ban would obviously apply worldwide. In a laconic statement Vettori had declared that he had let down the sport he loved, but above all, he had let down his wife and children. The name of the substance found in Vettori's urine had not been disclosed to the prying press, but Vettori's solicitor had deemed opportune to mention it was not a performance-enhancing drug.

'Yeah, yeah, yeah, same old story, really,' Ritchie grieved.

The next time Sheila barged into Ritchie's flat she was taken aback when she saw what looked pretty much like a firearm on his reclaimed teak coffee table.

'What the heck is that?' she said, gaping in utter shock.

'It's a Beretta Elite II, manufactured by Umarex and distributed in the United States by Umarex USA,' he quoted.

'I see...' she said.

'Its magazine holds four point five millimetres caliber BBs,' Ritchie explained, releasing the magazine from the butt of the pistol. 'It is powered by twelve gram CO2 cartridges, it is double action only, and has its statutory safety catch,' he said, sliding the catch on and off again.'

'Wow,' she mumbled, dropping her bag on the carpet and sinking down on her side of the sofa.

'It is an eighteen shot repeater, with a velocity of four hundred fifteen feet per second,' he recapped. 'Amazing isn't it?' And driving the magazine back in, started pulling the trigger. Of course the gun wasn't loaded, it only clicked empty, on and on.

'Could you put it away, Ritch?' she pleaded.

'It's not a real gun!' he shrieked. 'It's a replica, it shoots pellets!'

'Whatever! It must hurt anyway, real or not.'

'It might just give you a bruise, and make you bleed if shot at point-blank range, or if you are particularly unlucky, but it certainly won't kill you!' he said, and pointing the Beretta at her, he took aim, right between her eyes. Sheila backed off in the farthest corner of the sofa, drawing her knees high up in front of her, and shielding her face with both hands. He pulled the trigger once more, twice, trice, faster and faster, and a flurry of sharp clicks followed, as she squirmed and ground her teeth in distress.

'What did you buy this thing for?' She mustered the courage to ask him when he, at last, had put the weapon down on the table and joined her on the sofa.

'Things are happening all around us,' he said, frowning and throwing suspicious glances at the familiar surroundings – nothing however, he laid eyes on, led him to believe in the possibility of imminent danger, they were, after all, in the safe haven of his sitting room. 'Things that make me worry, and make me feel under threat, jeopardised, so I imagined I might as well get ready to face an assault.'

'With an air gun?' She gathered sneeringly.

'Yes, why not? It won't kill the assailants but at least it will scare them away,' Ritchie mulled over, fully immersed in his musings.

'I thought you were a Buddhist,' Sheila argued.

'I am,' he guaranteed, 'I am indeed, and believe you me, Buddha would only have to adhere to my standpoint, mine is a non-violent choice, it is a self-defence path I have picked by taking home this,' he said, pointing at the gun.

'Buddhist monks don't have guns though,' she brought up. 'Not even pellet guns.'

'First of all,' Ritchie particularized, magisterially raising his left index finger in mid-air, 'I am not a monk. In the second place, monks don't live in the urban jungle, as I do, bare a few exceptions. Finally, Buddha himself was, on three well-known occasions, the subject of assassination attempts, which goes to prove that nobody is immune from the envy and the malice gripping his neighbour's wicked heart. In such a bleak scenario, I'd rather like to be ready for the worst, just in case, if you don't mind,' he rebuffed.

The first plan to assassinate the Buddha was carried out when Devatta, a disciple who struggled to achieve nirvana, moved by envy, vowed to take his revenge on the spiritual leader. He appointed a man to kill Buddha, but the intricacy of the plot contemplated that the killer would then be killed by two other assassins, who in turn would be killed by four other people, ultimately slaughtered by eight other men. Nonetheless, when the appointed day came, the first killer flinched, he trembled before his inhumane task, and instead of carrying out the deed, he became a follower of Buddha. Actually, all the fourteen people involved in the killing cycle became disciples of their intended victim.

The second time around Devatta decided to put an end to Buddha's life all by himself. Thus when the Blessed One was passing under the Vulture's rock, Devatta, concealed high up on a peak right above the gully, rolled a boulder down from his hiding place. Providentially, the stone missed Buddha, it only struck against another stone, and the sparks that ensued, flying, injured the master's foot.

In the last try evil-bent Devatta made Nalagiri, a man-killer elephant, very drunk with alcohol, and then spurred him against Buddha. When Nalagiri saw Buddha he raised his trunk menacingly and charged him, but Buddha kept his cool, and stroked the elephant's trunk with such tenderness that the animal's fury was at once subdued, and its wilderness miraculously tamed.

Buddha's sanctity had proved unassailable, his inner peace was wholesome, undivided, rightfully attained, and therefore impervious to backstabbing and immune to ambushes. As for Ritchie, he had still a lot to learn, but where there is a will, there is a way.

Punctually, before the weekend, round about 9:00 p.m. on Friday, Lady Davina's call awoke him from the unfathomable depths of secret mantra Vajrayana practice, as he squatted enraptured, striving to generate a mind of emptiness with the heart of compassion.

'I am in Cambridge,' she said.

'Weren't you off to Canada?' He asked her.

'Yes, I am, in Cambridge, Ontario,' she explained. 'A nice little town with pitched roofs, spires, and a river, too. When streetlamps are on, in the evening, it almost feels as if we were in England.'

'Smashing!' He spewed.

'My son has been living here for quite a while now, he settled with a lovely Canadian girl.'

'Is he married?' Ritchie inquired, making an effort to show that he cared.

'No, not yet, but hopefully this might be the one person for him,' she reasoned. 'He's been in and out of relationships in the past, and never really found comfort. I am keeping fingers crossed,' she piped with unwavering voice. 'You know, London is only sixty miles away from me. London, Ontario, of course,' she quipped.

He giggled accordingly.

'Do you miss me a little?' Lady Davina said.

'I do,' Ritchie said warily, also rather untruthfully.

'Have you been seeing someone else?'

'Absolutely not! I haven't had much time on my hands.'

On occasion of his second date with Jess, Ritchie was wheedled into trudging, on Sunday evening, from Staverton Road to Brondesbury Park station, to meet her.

'It's just gonna be a ten, fifteen-minute walk,' she had cajoled him.

Jess seemed to be thoroughly obsessed with long-distance hikes, strolls in the park and suburban treks on residential side roads. She kept saying they should go to Hampstead Heath, one of these days, and blaming him for having never seen one of the city's best loved green spaces, even though he had been living in London for most of his adult life. In her view it almost compared to a crime. In clement weather she often cycled from Queen's Park to Hampstead, to the nursery, relatively early in the morning, cutting through the main traffic arteries, and cleverly skipping the rush hour, while keeping in shape at the same time. Sometimes she even hopped on foot to the workplace, she had owned up.

'If it's not raining it can be done quite easily,' she had contended.

Hence Ritchie took to march in north-easterly direction, at five on the dot, over pavements strewn with curled-up chippings of bark shed by the peeling plane trees. The slabs were cracked in places, as the trees had grown too tall and wide for the roadside settings in which they had been originally planted, and their roots longed to come out of their underground trenches. Dusk threw a veil of uncertainty, like a diaphanous mist, over the gables of the villas and mansions dotted on his right-hand side. Mercedes-Benzes, Toyotas and Bentleys were docilely parked in gated driveways. Some of the porches were guarded by marble lions and life-size terracotta warriors charged with the wearisome task of warning visitors of their masters' patent wealth.

Somewhere down the road he began peering into the deepening darkness, when someone approached him, as he sailed on, to be sure he wouldn't miss Jess. Until at last a damsel in red coat and woolly hat peered back at him, and gave him a wave.

'Hi! It's me,' Jess yapped.

'Hi, how are you?' He said.

'So, was it easy to find your way down here?'

'It was indeed, I only had to follow the road,' he said.

They were only yards away from shops, bars and restaurants now. She invited him to go for a drink into the nearest pub, a cavernous establishment with a black-and-gold facade and a vaguely old-fashioned, turn-of-the-century design – with a few oil lamps it would have looked like a pub from Victorian London.

'This time drinks are on me!' Jess made clear, for on their previous outing he had been buying.

She picked a quiet spot, between a settee and a table, in what gave the impression of being the eating area. A peppy waitress with a blonde, loose ponytail and a round-neck top jotted down their orders.

'I'll have a large glass of this... Primitivo,' Jess said, scrolling the wine list with her manicured forefinger.

'I'll have half a pint of cider,' Ritchie followed suit.

'How do you like this area then?' she asked as soon as they were alone again.

Ritchie cleared his throat, gave a cursory glance at the composition hanging on the wall to his left, it was a collage of matchboxes from days of old fitted in a rectangular, vertical frame, and conveying a fairly artistic potpourri of sensations, at length he said: 'yes, it is a lovely area, very trendy.'

'How long have you been living in this borough?' She pressed on.

'Ten years at least.'

'And you knew nothing about the existence of this high road?'

'Nope. Sorry,' he retorted, 'Never really went this far out.'

'Far out? This is your area!' She cried. 'You should know it like the back of your hand!'

A group of binge drinkers, meanwhile, in the corner by the window, grew louder by the minute. It appeared they were getting more and more boisterous proportionally to the quantity of alcohol they downed. As long as glasses were raised, so was the cacophony of their husky voices, in utter disregard of all the other customers wanting to enjoy a drink and a chat in an ear-friendly lounge.

Jess stared down at them and scowled. She was probably summoning up harsh curses, wholly forgetful, for once, of the Brahma Kumaris' ecumenical message of peace and love. She downed what was left of her wine, then, looking up at Ritchie, said: 'shall we go somewhere else?'

'Yes, of course!' He granted.

She took him into the pizzeria just around the corner, an eatery with all things Italian.

'I am dying for a pizza,' Jess said, snugly enthroned on the cherry-red leather banquette. 'Also, I must have a tiramisu, I am craving for it. I had a dream last night, the dessert was floating invitingly before my eyes,' she gave away, closing her eyes to rerun snippets of the appetising vision. 'I have been thinking about it all day long.'

'You are not pregnant, are you?' Ritchie said jocosely.

'Not that I know,' she said.

When they had had their Pizza and tiramisu, Jess took him into yet another pub, a more contemporary affair of stucco and brick wall. The rustic interior was festooned with raw black cables and plain light bulbs running the whole length of the ceiling and illuminating the remotest nooks and crannies. Only one corner of the spacious lounge lay in the penumbra, beyond the counter and bar, it was a mini living room, by the fireplace, complete with sofas and coffee table. Inevitably, she headed straight for the sofa nearest the dormant fireplace. He followed her in a rare mood of crestfallen obedience, as if Jess had hypnotised him.

'You see, I am not too sure I want to be in a relationship right now,' she said, sprawling on the settee, and reclining her head with the same sort of abandon she might have experienced during a one-to-one therapy session with the shrink. 'The last time I was in a relationship I was hurt, I was deceived,' she went on dreamily. 'After months it turned out this guy I was seeing was married, he had a family. My girlfriends were perplexed, they marvelled at the fact that I didn't even know where he lived, and they were right, I was a fool.'

'I am sorry to hear that,' he put in consolingly.

'On top of that I gave him three thousand pounds,' she said, 'he needed them badly, and I was only trying to help.'

She kept fidgeting with her long brown hair, driving her fingers through it like a comb, curling the ends by wrapping them around her index or middle finger while gazing in the distance, past the hanging lights, and the counter, past everything. Ritchie sipped absent-mindedly his second half-pint of cider, he had to twist his neck to look at her, as she spoke, and to soak up her grievance. He had stretched out his legs and the rest of his body as though he were in bed, instead than on a couch, at the boozer.

'Will you always be my friend?' She lipped lightly, distinctly, all of a sudden.

'Of course I will,' he solaced her. 'You can count on me. I really enjoy going out with you.'

Hardly had he said so than his phone gave him a buzz, it was a message alert. He took a peek at the screen, someone was apparently blowing him kisses, virtual ones, by sapient use of emoticons. He spied on Jess with the corner of his eye, not sure whether she had spotted the flirt or not.

'Is anyone trying to call you?' she said nonchalantly.

'No idea,' he minimised. 'It must be my brother.'

Thereupon he stole a glance at her own phone, which bore signs of incoming messages too.

'How about you?' he said, 'any messages?'

'Yes, perhaps from my brother,' she aped cheekily.

For a fistful of seconds they both busied themselves with a fair share of texting, before realising they were out on a date, and they were meant to talk to each other, not to third persons.

'Don't you ever think that there must something else to life?' she said, once phone fingering was over. 'I mean, the reason why I am going to these meditation classes is I'd like to find out who I am, I want to find my real self. Have you ever wondered who you really are?'

'I have indeed,' Ritchie acknowledged.

'I need guidance, and spiritual advice, I just can't cope on my own,' she went on, fiddling with the necklace now, and with its pendant, a heart-shaped charm studded with cubic zirconia gemstones. She truly came off as a soul in turmoil, affected by a mental anguish that required only God knows how many more sessions to be dissected, and overcome.

Upon getting ready to leave, Jess launched a desperate search for her woolly hat, which was nowhere to be found.

'Oh my God,' she whined. 'It was my favourite hat. How can I possibly have lost it? It was here one moment ago, I had it on when we came in, hadn't I?'

'I am pretty sure you did,' Ritchie concurred.

Eventually she had no choice but to bow to the inevitable, the hat was gone, it wasn't coming back. It was not there. She strolled out in the cold bareheaded and nonplussed, the loss having visibly contributed to ratchet up her anxieties, to dig deeper into the groove nibbled inside her by the worm of existential doubt.

She decided to walk him halfway up the road. On the corner with Winchester Road they stood for the final salutes, Jess' big brown eyes were wide open and glowing, either as a result of too much drinking or because of tiredness.

'So, shall we meet again next weekend?' she proposed.

'Yes, why not,' Ritchie said. 'I'll call you by Friday.'

She leaned heavily on him, and hugged him, to his great surprise, burying his face in the lush wave of her fluent chestnut-brown hair, and temporarily blinding him. Her embrace shielded him from the rest of the world, and all he could see and hear was her swishing waterproof coat.

To describe the following week as eventful would be a euphemism, an understatement. Cheltenham Festival was on, and the air was thick with excitement at the office. Excitement hovered in the room like a dense blanket of fog or other corporeal presence, like a condensation of all the fears, hopes, prayers, wishes and dreams of the gambling confraternity. On a misty afternoon of mid March John McDermot conducted, with measured gestures, the promising overture of the four-day horse racing spree, wiggling and paddling his plump, sausage-like pale fingers in front of the camera, his deerstalker solidly jammed on, his golden frame glasses perched on the tip of his pointy nose, his cape flapping by over a blue blazer and a white shirt secured at the neck by the leather bolo tie. His luxuriant, orangey sideburns, his tempers and tantrums, everything in his larger-than-life, exceeding figure, announced that the show was on in earnest. His petite, brunette assistant, Tamara, a clipboard firmly grasped to her chest, nodded her unconditional approval to all of his statements, however outlandish they may sound, at the same time leaguing up with him when an intruder, some bothersome time-waster or other, at the back, deemed opportune to invade the frame and wave idiotically his hi mum! In such eventualities – which were not infrequent – Tamara would quite simply close the gap between herself and McDermot, so that the camera, zooming in, could cut out of the frame all things unnecessary.

The betting frenzy that stormed the place on Tuesday was nothing short of frenetic, and high-octane. Cascades of ripped up slips dotted the blue carpet with white, confetti-sized scraps. Artan, Idriz, Uncle Tariq, Ritchie, the Chinaman, and even a Buddhist monk from the temple on Willesden Lane moved about feverishly, tipping off each other profusely and reciting their favourite horses' names mantra style. At three twenty the Champion Hurdle injected a new lease of life in all losers alike, and actually, for once, Ritchie and Artan managed to make a little profit, cashing in fifty quid apiece on Fagan's exhilarating victory. The party dragged on and on, until Friday, and even though, on balance, it couldn't be considered a totally lucrative venture, the staking orgy was, to our heroes, the equivalent of a life-saving defibrillation for the major shakeup it contributed to the restoration of their aspirations.

Raking up a couple of quid here and a fiver and a tenner there, on the wave of a four-fold lucky accumulator – one winner and three placed returned him seventy-nine pounds thirty-one pence – and one or two other cleverly crafted bets, Ritchie had just about managed to survive Cheltenham Festival unscathed, inflicting very little damage to his already depleted pockets. He had almost got out even. In celebratory mood, he rang up Jess on Friday evening.

'How was your week?' he purred self-complacently.

'It was hard work,' she whinged. 'The children were happy on Wednesday though, the playground was dusted with a thin layer of snow in the morning and they really enjoyed it.'

'Sounds great!' He figured. 'Are we going out this weekend, then?'

'Yes, indeed! Tonight I am babysitting, and tomorrow I am booked for a night out with the girls, but Sunday I am free, after five,' Jess worked out.

'Okay. Text me on Sunday afternoon to confirm, will you?'

'Fine, I will!' She promised.

Ritchie hung up.

Despite her heartfelt professions of friendship and love, on Sunday afternoon Ritchie waited for Jess' text in vain. He had been looking forward to their third date, it would have been, he reckoned, decisive, tilting the balance once and for all, and setting the tone for a deeper sort of bond, even one entailing intimacy perhaps. But his plans were cruelly shattered, they were wiped off like a child's sandcastle slapped and swallowed by the surf. Such was the disappointment he tried to drown it bringing on a new adventure. Scanning profiles on a dating site, he spotted, on Monday afternoon, what he thought was a comfortingly auspicious photo, of an Oriental girl lying alluringly in bed, in her profile picture, that was all it was needed to flick his switch. He messaged her at once, straightforwardly asking whether she was looking for a fun date. This deceptively simple hooking up technique that he had already employed in moments of utter despair – when his personal stable of thoroughbreds had been drastically dwindling – could be a lottery at times. It either worked instantly, or flopped badly – in the second eventuality he might even have to take some verbal abuse, which, however, being of the written kind, was rather diluted and way less cutting than if it had been dispensed orally.

Except than today the winds of good karma just happened to blow in his favour, and the Oriental girl, shortly after the bait had been fed her, replied that yes, she was up for it. He promptly proceeded to issue a formal invitation to his flat for the customary, lethal mix of pleasantries, wine and debauchery.

The Oriental girl texted him around five, giving him an appointment in one hour's time. They would meet outside West Hampstead station. By five to six he was firmly set in the foyer of the station, and ready to pick up his date. The stream of commuters flowed past the barriers in vigorous shoals, in and out, in both directions, and he had to step aside, backing into an alcove opposite the ticket machines, not to be engulfed and swept off his feet by the rush hour surge. On he waited, ten, twelve, fifteen minutes. At twenty past six she was not there, 'enough,' he sighed, and retraced his steps past the barriers and down the staircase, to the platform. As soon as he let himself back in his flat a text from the girl relayed that she had been only just around the corner while he had been waiting for her, a mere misunderstanding had kept them apart. He reiterated his invitation to join him at his place.

'Let me just take a half-hour break, to catch my breath, then I'll drive to your place,' she replied.

'Fine,' he conceded, and typed his full address.

When Amy – that was the improbable name the Far Eastern girl had given him – finally dropped by, holding a superior bottle of the finest Beaujolais, Ritchie's trepidation could hardly be contained. Directly the nectar was poured they nestled on the bumblebee-yellow sofa, and she took to sip and natter away.

'I divorced from my husband,' she said, 'he actually ran away with a younger girl and, well, ever since then I gave up monogamy altogether, it's outdated.'

It turned out this girl was far advanced in years, she was a middle-aged girl – her profile picture, as often is the case, must have been at least ten years old.

'Nevermind,' he ruminated to himself, 'still good going.'

Forty minutes and a lifetime of anecdotes later they kissed. She was beaming from ear to ear when their lips parted, and her eyes were sparkling. Presently she took charge of the situation, and started telling him what to do, directing the scene in a paroxysm of dictatorial fervor. Before he knew it, he had her middle finger worming its way up his ass.

In fairness he did try to contact Jess once again, around midweek. She said she regretted not having called him on Sunday, but the meditation class had been dragging on unexpectedly, plus she had been too tired later on to go anywhere else, so she had gone back home.

'We can do this coming weekend,' she tranquillised him, but to Ritchie her voice sounded off-key, and her assurances forcedly friendly, and rather insincere. He put down the phone and switched off the lights, found the best possible way to angle his head on the pillow and the countdown to oblivion began.

On Thursday morning, though, he awoke to a nasty surprise. Down there, on his penis, something unusual had appeared, it was a rash perhaps, or a tiny, pimple-sized swelling, anyhow it was clearly visible, right at the base of the shaft, on its underside. The fact that it wasn't in full view could be comforting to a degree, however, if he'd engage in sexual activities the bumpy bit would have been noticed sooner or later, and that worried him exceedingly. In addition to that the suspect of having contracted some kind of sexual disease poisoned his mind with brooding brainwork. The fear of having been transmitted an unmanageable infection made him tremble, and squirm with dread. Syphilis and chlamydia suddenly foisted themselves on his thoughts, like two obnoxious sisters coming forward arm in arm, and threatening lethal consequences, a lifetime of contamination, taxing itchiness, maybe more. He resolved to give the reddening lump some time to get lost, twenty-four, or even better, forty-eight hours, before resorting to drastic action.

Nevertheless, forty-eight hours later the blister was firmly set in place. It didn't seem to be budding, but neither gave the impression of being about to vanish. Occasionally it coloured, whereas at times of repose it whitened and flattened, but all in all it wasn't going anywhere. The immediate consequence of these new developments triggered a gnawing diminuendo in

115

Ritchie's otherwise unflagging self-esteem, especially on the side of his approaches to the gentler sex. All operations were suspended, no more messages and lecherous invitations were issued for several days. The repugnant idea of a career shattered by the tiniest pustule one could conceive augured to wreck all the progress made by dint of staunch determination. The blessings, the enlightenment, the spiritual growth so laboriously achieved, they would all be likely to cease sustaining his successful exploits in the amatorial field, and only because his penis had decided to go spotty. Understandably, the temptation to curse Amy, or whatever was her name, acquired new strength with each passing day, she must have given him that thing, it was her contact that had brought about the anomaly. She had made no secret of her vagaries and self-confessed promiscuity, and he must have fallen victim to her negligence and lack of restraint.

One week later the pimply bump showed no signs of remission. On getting out of bed, Ritchie picked the phone and dialled the number of Patrick Roberts Clinic. They gave him an appointment for two o'clock, on the following day. His lineaments were noticeably altered when he glided into the reception, at the hospital. His forehead was wrinkling on account of the extra load of worries that weighed on him. Still tests must be taken, facing the plain truth couldn't be postponed or circumvented any further. Once on the first floor he spelled out his name and address, at the reception desk.

'Take a seat, please. You will be called out soon,' said a fake blonde ebony lady, fluttering luscious fake eyelashes.

In the waiting room the TV was on, the flat screen was mounted on the wall. Three guys fidgeted and skimmed through lifestyle glossy magazines piled up on a shelf. They ogled him as he stepped in, before resuming their private conversation. A jacked-up brown fella flexed his biceps in a corner while flicking through the pages of his very own read of the day, making the paper look like a gym tool rather than a conveyor of culture. An Asian gent sat on the edge of his chair, by the window, looking out at the industrial landscape spreading beyond the hospital grounds; he was the first to be summoned into one of the examining rooms. Richie's turn came soon. He entered a small office where, perched on a swivelling chair at her desk and computer screen, yet another ebony lady questioned him regarding his symptoms. He told his story, of the casual encounter with Amy, and of the bubbly spot that was plaguing his sexual life and overcharging him with preoccupations. She asked him to pull down his trousers and underwear, so as to allow for a thorough examination of the ailing bits. After a good five-minute handling and squeezing she blurted out: 'there's some liquid in your testicles.'

'Is that bad?' Ritchie murmured.

The nurse kept silent, she went on manipulating his genitals with both blue rubber-gloved hands. He imagined that's how a cow must feel when it was milked. Immediately, upon completion of the nipping and clutching test, she posed a few more questions meant to establish a pattern in his sexual habits, insinuating, once it had been clear that there were no patterns whatsoever in his mating bouts, and that he was only driven, if anything, by haphazard incontinence, whether he had ever considered the opportunity of a regular, long-term relationship. He swore he was trying hard to find an arrangement of that sort.

Having been made to wait another fifteen to twenty minutes, Ritchie was then ushered into a different room, where a petite, blonde nurse – a real blonde this time –

collected his urine test tube. She also drew a sample of his blood, and performed a swab test – inserting a plastic probe into his urethra – and finally told him not to worry about his vesicle.

'It's just a cyst,' she winced disdainfully. 'It will soon go away.'

On Monday morning, the inevitable tete-a-tete with his work adviser brought about unforeseen winds of change. Ritchie was dispatched to the second floor, for apparently Mr. Delroy Williamson was not in the house – his ponderous girth must have been taken temporarily out of the jobcentre for training purposes. In substitution, a dreadlocked, spectacled, honey-tongued miss stepped in for him, making Ritchie an offer he certainly couldn't refuse.

'You will have to take part in a four-week work experience,' she put in quite simply. 'It's going to be very beneficial,' she added. 'Right now one of the main obstacles preventing you from getting a job is your lack of references, by taking part in this work experience programme you will gain new skills, and most probably references, too. Many of those who have gone through it have soon afterwards found work.'

Ritchie surrendered to the unequivocal governmental diktat. It was a matter of complying or dying as far as he could discern, as any refusal to meet the expectations would be sanctioned with financial penalties. His weekly dole was at stake, and the whole flimsy world he had been building around it could be severely undermined as a consequence of a single wrong move. No wonder, then, his spirits were low upon leaving Kilburn jobcentre. He hung his head in despair while shuffling up to the bus stop. Even though the sun was shining, and painting the high road with a cheerful yellowish light, his soul was heavy, clearly weighed down by a cogent sense of debacle.

Two days later, well past ten, he alighted on the deserted platform of Neasden tube station. The ticket office was shut, and the station was unmanned, therefore he couldn't even obtain one of those precious mini statements that entitled him to travel refund. Hence an underlying substratum of accumulated indignation vexed him already as he rang the buzzer of Daphnia House. At the reception a long-haired, ash-blonde boy in shirtsleeves looked him up over the counter. An electric guitar was being shredded in the background, its muffled sound came up in whiffs and waves from speakers half-hidden beneath the desktop. Ritchie was diverted to a first floor office, and was admitted to a corridor and to a spacious office with airy windows. Then he was motioned by a black girl in a red dress into an adjacent, cramped cubicle where a meeting table and chairs, a whiteboard and a couple of file cabinets left very little room for manoeuvre.

'The purpose of the work placements we provide,' the wary employee began once jobseekers had taken their seat at the table, 'is to make sure you give something back to the community.'

Moans of bitter contention arose from the four corners of the tight space, the dissensus was unanimous.

'You will be asked to devote some of your time to unpaid work, to be carried out in charities of our choice,' the black girl envisaged. 'It's pretty simple, really. As for the type of work we will provide you with, right now there are some gardening, kitchen porter, and customer service roles available, and that's what you will be asked to do basically, for six hours a day, five days a week. Any questions?'

The recriminations of the mob grew louder, inordinate, the unemployed bunch were disgruntled. So much so that the assembly was dissolved sooner than expected.

'You will receive a letter explaining everything about your duties and place of work, within seven days!' The black girl warned before the riotous troupe deserted the meeting room. Then Ritchie and his partners in misadventure filed out fuming and desolate.

'How's the staphylococcus faring?' Ritchie hooted down the phone in the evening.

'He's dormant apparently,' Janet Barker said airily, 'but there's more coming. Josh has been diagnosed with an inguinal hernia!'

'No way! How did that happen?'

'He's always lifting stuff, at work, and that brings it out, according to doctor Mangnall,' mum explained. 'Plus he drives the scooter, daily, and the rubbing with the seat might have helped too.'

'I see. Is there a solution to the problem?'

'An operation is recommended only if the hernia causes severe or persistent symptoms, or in case any serious complications develop. We'll wait and see, I suppose.'

'I'll be keeping fingers crossed for him,' Ritchie said.

When mum rang off, he lit the candles laid on a white flat ceramic plate on his coffee table, folded his legs up on the edge of the sofa and began: 'Just like myself all my kind mothers are drowning in samsara's ocean; o so that I may soon release them, bless me to train in bodhicitta. By pacifying my distractions and analysing perfect meanings, bless me to quickly gain the union of special insight and quiescence. When I become a pure container through common paths, bless me to enter the essence practice of good fortune, the supreme vehicle, Vajrayana. May those who guide me on the good path, and my companions all have long lives; bless me to pacify completely all obstacles, outer and inner.'

As he intoned the healing prayer, a ginger cat, straying from the neighbours' house, landed on the outer ledge of his window and took to peer at him through the glass pane, meanwhile a magpie and a blackbird fought over breadcrumbs someone had strewn on the roof of the garden shed over which his flat looked, and the cat's attention was soon drawn to the feathered squabble.

The numerous, insistent objections of animal welfare organizations had induced, over the years, Aintree racecourse officials to improve veterinary facilities. In 2008, a new surgery was erected in the stable yard, a state-of-the-art treatment box equipped with an X-ray unit, video endoscopy, equine solarium, and sandpits. For horses requiring more specialist care, ambulances were made available, allowing, under police escort, immediate transport to the Philip Leverhulme Equine Hospital. Moreover, five vets were placed on standby alongside the racetrack during the running of the race so that they may provide immediate basic treatment for injured fallers at the fence, and even more vets were stationed on the finishing post and in the surgery.

The Grand National was charged, this year, with a whole new set of nostalgic nuances, as Tony McColls, multi-awarded Champion Jockey, Jump Jockey of the Year, Jockey of the Year, Jump Ride of the Year, winner of Grand National, Gold Cup, Champion Chase, Champion Hurdle, King George, Ryanair Chase, RSA Chase, Fighting Fifth Hurdle, Tingle Creek, Arkle, Welsh Grand National, Scottish Grand National, Midlands Grand National, Irish Grand National, Lexus Chase, Galway Plate, BBC Sports Personality of the Year in 2011, appointed MBE in the 2003 Queen's Birthday Honours, and last but not least, winner of three Guinness World

121

Records in 2012, had made public this would be his very last appearance in the historic handicap steeplechase.

'The greatest jump jockey of all time has announced he will retire in two weeks,' John McDermot plaintively put, twitching under his cream-coloured Stetson and drawing circles in the air with both hands, faithfully assisted by clipboard-clenching Tamara. 'How sad is that? I dare say. How frustratingly depressing... McColls has under his belt more than sixteen thousand races, in a career that spanned over twenty years, seeing him victorious on more than four thousand three hundred occasions. How good is that?'

The hi mum wavers had soon gathered right behind bulky McDermot and sinuously complacent Tamara, and the customary flurry of salutes and camera tilting dodging had ensued unperturbed, unmoved by the pundit's emotional appeal.

At ten to three the cameras peeped into the weighing room. Ritchie and Artan, eyes glued to the screen high up on the wall, were treated to a revealing intrusion on McColls' last instants before being summoned to the scales, as he sat rigidly on his portion of bench, staring right ahead rather unseeingly, his face tautened by the tension. In terms of placing their bets they hadn't made up their mind yet, for once it had been agreed between them they should try their luck separately.

'This way if ill-luck is bent on taunting one of us the other may still have a chance,' Ritchie had mooted convincingly.

The Chinaman, at the farthest end of the row of linked blue chairs, hunched over a miniature laughing Buddha statuette, and stroked the amulet's belly with his forefinger, entrusting his unfaltering faith to the money-earning properties of the monk's effigy.

At five past four jocks were assembled for the ritual group photo. Thirty-nine chaps in bright-coloured silks sat or stood in triple row, smiling nervously and chatting right and left, as happy snappers, paparazzi and pros alike immortalised the clash of oranges, blues, yellows, greens, and reds making up the higgledy-piggledy motley rainbow. There seemed to be no distinction whatsoever between them, and yet, in that cheerful ensemble lurked a winner, only a single one of them would be crowned champion today, to come second or third would be pretty much irrelevant.

Twelve past four, jocks mounted, paraded proudly in front of the stand. Two minutes later riders and horses headed for the start. To familiarise his horse with the task lying ahead, one of the jockeys had taken him near the first fence, to have a long, scrutinizing look at it. The animal had given away a jolly good dose of insecurity though, 'do you really expect me to jump that?' were the words that best translated the quadruped's compulsive head bobbing, had he been able to voice them.

Eighteen past four, they were off. At the first fence Ennui, Ruby Red, Ellis Own and Moonriver were down. Wee Bit Fancy was in the lead. The thirty-five galloping contenders left on the track dashed past like a cavalry charge, great divots were impetuously kicked up in the air, the drumming rumble of hooves transmitted to all those who were anxiously watching, in the betting shop, a strange sensation of apprehension, rhythmically beating a tempo much in tune with the thuds of overexcited hearts. Kaspar King fell at the eight fence. Rocky Crest nosed in right behind the leaders. At the thirteenth fence the wild bunch jumped smoothly, Many Doubts was in there, and so was Just Cause and Ocean Sea. They were coming up at the Chair now, one more effort and, voila, everyone was safe and sound on the other side, and still in the race.

No major accidents so far. As the second circuit began, most of the horses were still standing, then Monkey Business pulled up, soon after Lieutenant and Nemo were pulled up also, at the Canal Turn two more horses were down and out, McColls was second, and doing well. Trader fell, oohs of wonder and disappointment ran around the room. Two fences to go. Many Doubts was leading, Schooner and McColls were still second, All Saints was third. 'Who will win?' was the question teetering on everyone's mind. It surely must be decided between the three of them, but then Monsoon crept steadily up to the trio. Many Doubts came up to the elbow. He was tiring, but held on tight, and yes, he made it, he had just won the Grand National.

Artan was on the floor, all the gamblers in the room turned their eyes on him, he was having what might have looked like a seizure, grasping his ticket in the right hand held high up and wheeling and pivoting on his left hip while down on the ground, his fourteen pounds black blazer mopping up all the dust and debris entrapped on the carpet.

'I won,' he bellowed, 'I won.'

Indeed he had. Staking fifty quid on twenty-five to one Many Doubts had returned him the handy sum of one thousand two hundred fifty pounds. Not bad for an afternoon at the bookies. Yes, he had won.

There was more music and song that night, at the Kosovar refugees' retreat, behind closed doors, prudently, but with all their pride intact, and plenty of cans of lager for the entire clique, which were piled up in an impressive stash the morning after, empty and partially squeezed, in the green recycling box for the neighbourhood to see there had been no sparing of expenses to celebrate Artan's resonant coup.

Persuaded by the overwhelming significance of statistics, according to which the ninety-four per cent of the population was deemed to be Buddhist, and even the king was constitutionally urged to be Buddhist and the upholder of the faith, Ritchie wondered whether he had to look at Thailand, the Land of Yellow Robes – the garments of choice of Buddhist monks – to take decisive steps on his journey of purification. Therefore, when Nop, his latest flirt, told him she was from Bangkok, he wasted no time, and asked her out pronto on Friday evening.

She was twenty minutes late, sauntered placidly out of Notting Hill Gate station, came toward him, surveyed him with an appraising eye, then flashed a welcoming smile. Her English, though, was indisputably substandard, hence Ritchie had to repeat each of his sentences at least twice, have one regular-speed go at it, and then replay the same phrase, or a shortened version of it, at a much slower pace, often making additional stops to give out vocabulary definitions of the words she could not get, or to facilitate their comprehension coming up with a synonym or two. Basically the first half-hour was spent according the girl a free language lesson, with the result that by the time they had reached the viaduct, to the north end of Portobello Market, he was incredibly tired, thirsty, and out of breath. It had grown dark too, and all he had managed to elicit from his date was the broken narrative of her clumsy attempt at working as a waitress in a Thai restaurant, where her lack of skills and poor fluency in English had soon showed, making the sacking inevitable.

'I wanted to try to work with dogs, to take them to the park,' she said, 'but it's not enough money. Only two hours' work per day. Not enough!' She wept.

Ritchie could have set her mind at rest referring to his own search for the final release from the alternate effects of karma, a search that gave new shape and size, at once, at everything that wasn't part of the progress, of the spiritual pilgrimage toward enlightenment, making all mortal vicissitudes appear insignificant in comparison, and material goals like lacklustre equivalents of mere inanimate objects, of forms deprived of substance, of essence. What he said instead was, it was already hard to find a job if you spoke English, no wonder then she was struggling so much, it was natural, understandable.

Nop's hair was long and black, sleek and silky, parted with great care in the middle, and that took a few years off her real age, her slim figure and flat stomach, as well, made of her a slightly past-her-prime teenager. Her voice was thin and papery, but as she faltered and stumbled on words there were less chances it would come across as a persistent, unpalatable wail.

Noticing they were straggling not far from it, Ritchie proposed they'd have some food in the Malaysian canteen Sheila was so fond of. Nop nodded approvingly. When they got there he held the door open for her, and in she sashayed. At the counter a good choice of pre-cooked dishes in metallic trays invited them to pick and mix.

'I am going to heat the food up for you,' said the guy on the other side of the counter, patronisingly. He must have been the owner of the place, or a member of the family that owned it.

Nop pointed at a pyramid of spicy rice, Ritchie insisted on adding some chick peas in a red sauce that promised a challenge for his ultra-sensitive taste buds, and thus their full plate of food was garnered, microwaved, handed over. They sat in a quiet corner, under a Malaysian flag pinned to the budget wood panelling, just above a rectangular mirror. Ritchie scooped up the chick peas and scanned the headlines on a copy of the Evening Standard left lying on the table while his date gobbled up the rice and checked her phone. Nirvana must not be too far away, he sensed.

The only downside of his otherwise pleasant evening out with Nop was the excruciating pain that had slowly but surely got hold of Ritchie's left foot. The Thai girl had complained also, protesting that their stroll had been going on for too long – she had done so shortly before he had invited her to make the pit stop at the canteen – that was too much walking in one day for her taste, no doubt, besides, the grey leather boots she was wearing were all but comfortable. In the wake of her outcry his attention had been drawn, instinctively, to his own feet, and he had then realised that a propagating ache was straining him, like a burning sensation, as if the sole of his left foot was being overheated on the crest of invisible flames. The spasms had kept plaguing him during the night, even as he lay in bed, and the foot should have been feeling better, once it had been taken off the ground and granted several hours of absolute rest, whereas it ailed, instead, with cramps and persistent, stabbing twinges.

The morning after there were no improvements whatsoever, and so the one after that, and the next one, and the one following the next, to the point that Ritchie deemed wise to inform the jobcentre about these unforeseen circumstances. Uninvited, he popped in on Wednesday, at ten o'clock – the jobcentre opened at ten on this day only, to let valued staff members discuss all the issues that mattered in one-hour long meetings – and was steered in with a crowd of impatient customers that had all been waiting outside for a while and seemed to be hankering for an audience. Once he had landed on the first floor, he was told to seat down and cool his heels until the manager would be ready to see him.

Ten to fifteen minutes later, an Eastern lady beckoned him over to her desk. Her name badge read: Anoushka, manager.

'I am having a problem with my left foot,' Ritchie said, having hobbled from the sofa to the chair planted before the manager's workstation. 'I am not sure I will be able to attend the work experience programme,' he added, 'I mean... Not if the type of work I will be required to do involves standing up for many hours.'

'Have you been to the doctor?' Anoushka asked, eyeing him up through the red-frame opticals. 'We need to see a sick note before dispensing you from duty.'

'You see,' he grieved, 'I might be able to sit down at the desk and fill spreadsheets all day long,' he gave an explicative nod at the computer screen she was constantly staring at, as though solutions to every problem would suddenly spring out of it, 'but not be able to stand or walk around.'

'Sure,' Anoushka replied. 'Bring us the sick note and we'll take you off the work experience.'

On the Friday Ritchie had been out with the Thai girl something weird had occurred. Around half past eleven, while he was sprawled on the bed, an email had reached his inbox, from the bank, apparently. He had been prompted to click on a link attached to the email and redirecting him to the official website of the bank, where he was asked to fill in the blanks with the code numbers he used to do online banking, his telephone number, even his national insurance number. The whole operation, at this time of the day, sounded slightly off-key, and yet the fear that he wouldn't be able to accede his account any longer, had he not complied with the intimations of the reminder, induced him to do as told, despite the tingling sense of foreboding that heightened his anxiety. Right after the series of digits had been entered, each in the allocated space, he had turned off the lights and readied for departure, blissful sleep had soon dissipated all his apprehensions.

During the weekend he had been withdrawing cash from the ATM on the high road, as usual, for the minute shopping, and everything had gone down without a hitch. It was with sincere bewilderment then that he recoiled when, the following Thursday, he was told by the bank clerk, as he slotted his card into the machine, in order to pay the rent, that for some reason the transaction was being denied.

'There must be something wrong with the card,' the vampish lady behind the counter dryly informed him. 'Can you see the manager, please?'

The bank manager, a spectacled young fellow in a dark suit, escorted him into his boot, where private matters would be more likely to remain so, had him comfortably seated on a conference cushioned chair, then had a look at the computer screen to try and find out what had gone wrong.

'Your security codes have been breached,' he hinted. 'I have to call the security team for this to be sorted out.'

'Fine,' Ritchie said, 'go ahead.'

'Do you mind speaking to them?' The manager soon bade, holding out the receiver.

'Hello, Mr. Barker,' a woman's mellow voice shrilled at the other end of the line. 'Somebody has tried to transfer sixty pounds from your account to a NatWest account, are you responsible for this transaction?'

'I am not,' he stated, 'it wasn't me.'

'We thought so, in fact the transfer was blocked immediately. The same person has then tried to transfer a larger sum, six thousand pounds, on to the same account, even this second transaction was not allowed.'

'I don't have six thousand pounds,' Ritchie protested. 'Anyway, has any cash been taken out of my account at all?'

'Not at all Mr. Barker. However, your card has been blocked, and our team will have to conduct the appropriate investigations. Is that going to be okay with you?'

'Sure, if this is the procedure, only I am worried about having to cope without my bank card.'

'It won't take long Mr. Barker, we will keep you informed over the phone.'

'You see,' Ritchie butted in, 'I am having problems with the phone, too. It seems to have no signal right now.'

'No worries, we will get in touch by post.'

It was strange indeed, that his phone had stopped working shortly after his reply to the harmful Friday night email. Once he had done with the bank manager, Ritchie reckoned he should pay a visit to the phone company store. In the olive-green shop a tall, black, bearded clerk dialled the magic number summoning a troubleshooter wizard and passed on the handset to Ritchie. He was then informed somebody had called and requested a deactivation of the SIM card. Clearly a pattern emerged from all these uncanny coincidences, the fraudster must be pulling the strings of Ritchie's life from the unperturbed safety of his hiding place, backstage, like a mad puppeteer, malignantly bent on stealing his identity. The unexpected disappearance of his adviser, in the jobcentre, led him to believe there could be a connection between these latest events. Girthy Williamson was nowhere to be found, and in Ritchie's vivid memory the moment the extra-large chap had scratched with his inky pen tip the numerals making up his bank account sprang to mind as a reminder that nobody else but him knew about his savings and finances, obliged as he was by the Department for Work and Pensions to keep a vigilant eye on Ritchie's assets. Who else had been regularly checking his bank statements, to make sure no other entries than the dole were recorded on it, and that he wasn't exceeding the limits within which he'd be entitled to claim the benefits? More to the point, the fact that he had been required to reveal his national insurance number, by the cowardly emailer, established a definite link between Williamson and the attempted fraud, in Ritchie's flustered state of mind.

'How could you be so ingenuous to give them your code numbers?' Rebuked Janet Barker, glad destiny had given her a chance to knock him down, at last.

'Yeah, the website looked exactly like the bank's, mum, how could I know?'

'It serves you right! Next time you won't be fooled again, hopefully.'

'I won't click on any dodgy link, ever again!' Ritchie promised.

As for the tiny swelling on his private parts, despite the nurse's reassurances that it would soon be flattened and go away, it had instead shown a galling resilience. The results of his tests came in, it was all good news indeed, everything clear, no sexual diseases so far, but the boil was there, and he hadn't had sex since it had first bubbled up. Action must be taken. Ritchie dug up from his bathroom cabinet a miraculous gel that destroyed any imperfection of the skin after a few days' application. The remedy was aimed at warts and verrucas especially, on the other hand he imagined it would have worked anyhow, as all it did was burn the layers of skin where the pernicious growths had taken root, and therefore wipe all blemishes neatly out. He thought the salicylic acid might as well be given a chance, what could possibly go wrong? At worst his penis may have been superficially scraped. Without further ado he squeezed a drop or two of amber-coloured gel on to the ailing spot, waited a couple of minutes for it to harden, and form the crust underneath which the erosion process was tripped, then put all his hanging bits back in the briefs and the trousers and looked forward to a brighter, unblemished future of more how's your father.

It took several calls to the service provider to restore his phone line. Ritchie paid a few more visits to the olive-green store, and was punctually told the SIM card would be up and running in a matter of hours, but then disappointingly the much-awaited fixing failed to materialise. Until he yielded to a young shop assistant's suggestion that he'd purchase a new SIM card, it would cost him five pounds only, the paltry sum would actually be accredited to his number, so he'd lose nothing, really.

'Okay then,' Ritchie said, 'let's buy the new card.'

No sooner had he capitulated to the chap's promotional offer than a new, more expensive deal was outlined.

'How about switching to our broadband?' The black-haired, clean-shaven boy threw in temptingly. 'May I ask how much you pay per month?'

Ritchie disclosed the details of his existing deal.

'Well, if you switch to us you'll save at least seven pounds per month, for the first six months,' the boy calculated convincingly.

'What about the following six months?'

'For the next six months you'll pay what you are already paying now!'

'Uhm, I see.'

'Plus, you'll have to pay fifty pounds for the installation.'

'Which means that even for the first six months, once you spread the fifty pounds across them, I'll end up paying just as much as I am doing already,' Ritchie topped off.

The boy went quiet. Finally, he said: 'When your new card will start working you should receive a text, you'll also be asked to give me a score, evaluate the assistance I gave you today, will you give me ten out of ten?'

'Sure,' Ritchie vowed, 'if the card works I'll give you ten out of ten!'

The boy pointed at his name badge, on the olive-green polo neck shirt bearing the company's logo.

In a few days' time the salicylic acid had done a good deal of skin abrasion. A minuscule crater stood now where the swelling had previously been solidly rooted, however the bottom of the crater was red and sore, the more the gel eroded the layers of skin, the more the spot threatened to turn into a pustule, and a light discharge of pus soon ensued from it.

On Thursday morning, at half past eight, Ritchie joined the queue outside Doctor Rajagopal's practice to be admitted to the walk-in surgery. Mrs. Jones was in the queue as well, ahead of him, she was arched over her crutches, grasping the handles with her bony, spotted, greenish hands, her face hidden for the curve that bent her spine, forced to look down, groundwise, perusing each single slab of the pavement, as she crept forward, through the magnifying glass of her oversized spectacles, like a quadruped rather than a biped. She could have passed for one of those malnourished cows wandering along the shores of the river Ganges, or in those slums that, albeit poverty-stricken, still venerated the animal as a sacred one, and let it roam free, unharassed. Probably that's what she had been, Ritchie fantasised, in her previous life, a holy cow, and the transmigration into human form had been the prize awarded her for all her virtues. Her daughter, the sole person in the whole wide world who could occasionally still take care of her, was obviously busy at work, and so the old lady had to rely on the compassion of the neighbourhood to be ushered in and out of places, helped to climb up and down staircases, or for anything else her way-too-frail frame wasn't able to master.

A sari-clad, brownish lady with a gold nose stud flanked her at present, making sure she won't tumble face down for too much bending forward.

'My daughter would have come,' Mrs. Jones screeched feebly, 'but she has to be at the office by nine.'

The brownish lady nodded and held Mrs. Jones' left arm, right above the elbow, so as to steady her up – despite the four legs supporting her, she was anything but unwavering, all four limbs appeared to be shaky in fact, and the trembling was transmitted, by contagion, to all those who, for one reason or another, got anywhere near her.

Just as the sliding door of the Medical Centre glided open, and the queue was unhurriedly swallowed indoors, inching in little by little, and settling on the stairs and in the corridor leading to the reception, Mrs. Jones and her momentary chaperone headed for the platform lift but, no matter how strenuously they pressed the button, the door would not open.

'Can someone tell the reception that the lift is out of order, please?' squawked Mrs. Jones.

Voice must have been spread, down the queue, about it, but an answer never came back. Therefore, the old lady set out to stumble over the stairs, one step at a time, with the solicitous backing of her brownish sidekick.

Soon the waiting room on the first floor was packed, having confirmed their name and date of birth, patients were crammed into the little lounge opposite the reception. At nine o'clock they all flocked to the surgery, upstairs, and to a larger lobby with a greater number of seats. Mrs. Jones had managed to scramble up the first two flights of stairs, and from then on had been taken up by the lift. She dragged herself into the seating area, and scarcely had she parked her scraggy rump into one of the chairs of the first row than Annette, a blonde, youngish-looking neighbour just come by, took over from the sari-clad lady as her caretaker.

'They will never find out who killed Steve,' the old lady wailed as her younger friend sat down to her left.

'I think it was his brother, Ian, who did it, he must have poisoned him after Barbara's farewell party, when they were all alone in the pub,' said Annette.

'How about Rob, his nephew, it could have been him as well,' Mrs. Jones objected.

'Yes, that could be true, but Ian has never got over the fact that Steve married Laura. She was his childhood sweetheart, he resented that.'

'We will see,' the old lady chewed on, 'it will be revealed in the next few episodes.'

'Yeah, I am always falling out with mum, at seven, because she wants to watch Northern Dale, in the sitting room, and I have to strain my back and my eyes staring at the fourteen-inch screen, in the kitchen, to watch Londoners, slouching on a hard chair, like a charlady.'

Mrs. Jones chuckled sonorously. Ritchie meanwhile, had found a seat in the second row, next to a hijab-wearing woman and her two children, a boy and a girl. The girl hung coyly around mum, hugged her, hid her face under mum's wings, whereas the boy was a wee bit more adventurous. He could hardly sit still and mucked noisily about. Ritchie grew restless, the child was too close for comfort and his lack of discipline put him on high alert. In point of fact his fears were shortly confirmed when the kid, bending forward, threw up copiously on the cheap light-blue laminate. A man-made pool of green-yellow soup stood now where the boy's feet had previously dwelled. Ritchie made sure his black leather shoes hadn't been hit by the smelly tsunami. Splashes hadn't travelled so far apparently, then he moved gingerly one seat down the row, next to an adult, a lady pensioner, intending to be safer. The boy's mum went about gathering absorbent paper sheets from a dispenser up on the wall and proceeded to drain the artificial pool while her daughter held on to her legs like a frightened chick. Ultimately peace and quiet were restored, and the display announcing in red characters the name of the next patient to be seen became once again the centre of everyone's attention.

Ritchie's turn came eventually. Doctor Rajagopal was giving instructions to a nurse in dark-blue uniform when he set foot in the office.

'Sure, doctor, it will be done!' Jawed the spectacled nurse, nodding and about-facing to leave.

'How can I help you Mr. Barker?' the doctor said, motioning for him to take a seat.

'Well, I am having a problem with my left foot, doctor,' he began. 'It all started a week ago or thereabouts, I went for a long walk, something I hadn't done for a while, and as a result my foot hurts.'

'Was it a mountain hike you went for?'

'Not really, I just strolled about in Portobello Road, for a couple of hours though.'

'I see, and how would you describe the pain?'

'I'd say it is like a burning sensation, spreading from the sole, and going up, up, up, sometimes as far as the knee. The pain feels like a series of sharp stabs, it goes on even at night, and actually is keeping me awake, making sleep uncomfortable.'

'Can I see the foot?' the doctor said.

'Yes, sure,' he agreed, and undid his shoe laces, rolled down his sock and lifted the leg so that his foot could be admired at ease.

'It doesn't seem to be swollen,' she observed.

'Indeed, there is nothing wrong at first sight, it hurts though, badly,' he emphasised.

'What shall we do about it?'

'I have no idea, I came here to be advised for the best,' he went on. 'If you could write me a sick note, that would help, as I am not in condition to walk or stand for many hours at a time right now.'

'Okay, I will write you a note,' the doctor vouchsafed, and typed on the two-page form a few words about the nature of the ailment, in the appropriate box, printed it and handed it over.

Ritchie folded the document carefully, placed it down on his side of the desk, ready for collection before he'd be going, then added: 'oh, doctor, there's another little thing that is bothering me. A swelling, on my penis. I have been to the Patrick Roberts Clinic, they said it was nothing to worry about, a cyst. The fact is, as I noticed it wasn't deflating I applied some warts gel on it, and now the area is sore.'

'Shall we take a look at it?' the doctor urged.

He pulled down his trousers and briefs. Doctor Rajagopal donned white antiseptic gloves, picked a pre-labelled tube and a bud, and asking him to expose the diseased part, gently rubbed the bud over it.

'This is called swab test,' she filled him in. 'It will tell us if there's an infection. For the time being I will prescribe an ointment that will heal the skin.'

Ritchie was much relieved upon walking out of the Medical Centre. A punctilious onlooker might have sworn there was a faint limp in his step, but his spirits were certainly higher now than a couple of hours earlier.

Five days on he met Nop for the second time, same place same time. He worked hard not to let his pain show, and to contrive an unfaltering stride. It was windy, blustery, and cool. Forceful westerly gales of up to sixty miles per hour swept Notting Hill Gate as if it were a thoroughfare for gusts at play. Trees were shaken, branches bent under the blows, leaves ripped off and flung up in the air, or chased on the pavement and scattered all over the driving lanes.

'Oh, my God! My hair!' Was the first thing Nop blundered out when she emerged from the tube station.

Ritchie led her down the road, cheering her up.

'There is a nice pub, just around the corner,' he said.

They had to wrestle the wind to make their way to the watering hole's doors.

'Aaargh!' She groused, 'I am scared. I am going to fly away!'

Having managed to trudge onward, Ritchie pushed through the heavy wooden doors of the Hillgate, held them open until his date had reached safety, then took to scour the place for a seat, but there weren't any, it was packed.

'We must try somewhere else,' he said to Nop, who had been trailing him pawing on softly on the creaky floor boards.

She looked grim, pulled a face, the idea of being whipped up again by the lashing airflow did not appeal to her. Out they went, and back to the main road, then, heading north, they waded all the way to Portobello Road, despite the tenacious opposition of the disorienting blasts.

Before long the dating birds found refuge at The Duke of Wellington. They ordered drinks at the counter – the usual half a pint of cider for Ritchie and a half of lager for her – had a quick peep around, then settled in a cosy, adjoining room, half-empty but for another couple chatting animatedly and two guys enjoying after-work pints. Right in the middle of the round table, next to a slim vase and a single, withering, purplish Gerbera daisy, on the standing menu the Duke of Wellington, in blue uniform with golden epaulettes and extra-large cocked hat, sliced the world with his sabre, Sunday roast fashion.

'I like it in here,' Nop drawled, taking in the gilt mirror on the mantelpiece, the divan, and the vista on the street at a glance. 'Much better than the place where I live.'

'Do you live in a shared house?' Ritchie assumed.

'Yes, the landlords live in the house with us. They are so stingy!' She piped. 'We have to buy everything, toilet rolls, washing up liquid... In the morning I must wake up at six to go to the bathroom and wash, and do my hair, before my housemates go in.'

Her sleek black hair was her pride and joy. She put a lot of effort into the daily care of it, and indeed, hadn't been for its almost unnatural sheen, she would have been quite plain, even bland perhaps, in terms of looks.

'Before I lived with a Thai family, but it was worse, they had things to say whatever I did, if I spent half an hour in the bathroom they complained, if I watched the TV in their room they complained.' She flashed fleeting full smiles as she spoke, and a crease on the right side of her mouth surfaced that could be almost compared to a dimple.

The evening was drawing to a close. Ritchie's expectations had been rocketing ceiling high as his date grew more and more familiar with him. He had been secretly savouring the prospect of an intimate climax while being wholeheartedly transported by Nop's still-life sketches.

'Will I see you again?' he insinuated, just as they were back outside Notting Hill Gate station.

'Maybe,' she wept.

'I thought we could go to my place one of these days.'

'I don't know. I don't want to go to your place.'

'No? Why not?'

'I am not sure,' she fussed about, 'I don't know if I like you that much!'

Ritchie stood petrified, not sure if he had to laugh or brood over the blunt remark. So much for kindness and compassion. According to the Dalai Lama, and based on biological reasons and on their ability to give birth, women are, by nature, more compassionate than men. Had the majority of world leaders been women the danger of wars and aggressive policies would be reduced by a great deal, the holy man had once warned in a public speech. Now this was singular, wasn't it? That he must bump into the only Thai and Buddhist female specimen that had taken no hint from the spiritual leader and had chosen not to abide by these precepts inspired by universal, unconditional love and peace, he reflected despondently on his way back home.

He had barely set foot in his flat than a message from Nop was delivered.

'Will you go out with me again?' She texted.

Ritchie was startled, he had been trying to convince himself, during the half-hour commute home, that forgetting the entire episode would be the best course of action available to him. Obviously Nop's last minute reconsideration threw him off balance, he was lost for words. Anyhow he texted back: 'sure, when are you free?'

'Maybe next week? I'll let you know.'

'Fine, I'll be looking forward to it.' He typed, although this last sentence was put down rather mechanically, without giving it much thought.

Toward the end of the week yet another message roused Ritchie from his meditations on the final destination of man's soul, from Lady Davina, who routinely inquired about his plans for the weekend.

'I am not fit for walking or going out at all, I am afraid.' He admitted.

'I am really sorry to hear that. I hope you get better soon, we will meet another time,' she returned.

Uncle Tariq's recycling mission scope could also be compared, for its all-encompassing breadth, to a Buddhist monk's journey toward emancipation and light. In time, his early morning rounds saw him pushing the boundaries of the exploratory trips well beyond the confines of the rows of terraced houses laid out in the immediate proximity of the family retreat. Like a novel Marco Polo, he tramped on to the four corners of the borough, dragging along his faithful two-wheeler, a fag eternally propped between his lips – the burning beacon leading the way to the junk route, just as well as Polo's scouts and fellow merchants had shown him the way to the silk route.

The class of items he ended up trolleying home, too, was subjected to a gradual, sifting process, and whereas initially he had been yielding to a frenetic, feverish impulse to carry away as much as he could, a definite shift from quantity to the quality of the treasure troves deserving collection had taken place of late in his refining mind. The domestic appliances, most valued by Idriz and company for being right at the top end of the scale on account of their high commercial value, which in turn made bartering them at the Cash Generator a piece of cake, were more and more often overlooked by the old geezer, whose keen eye fell instead on objects that, albeit artistically or emotionally more engaging, were of little or no value at all. A blue porcelain Yorkshire Terrier, the muscly action figure of a wrestler, a fin de siècle telephone, chipped ceramic plates and wobbly teapots, a stuffed squirrel in a rampant pose, a square wooden clock, a shell-shaped pewter ashtray – it was pretty much impossible for an inveterate smoker to resist the fatal attraction of an ashtray – a Spalding tennis racket hailing from the seventies, a yellow pot, two purple stem glasses, a stringless, bruised classic guitar, a miniature, portable chess board, and a plaster bust of Beethoven, all were safely lugged back home, but the apotheosis of Uncle Tariq's career as junk collector was surely attained when he found a life-size human skull and, not knowing whether it was real or sham, but thoroughly thrilled under the effect of the spell it had cast on him, holding it in his left hand – the right being busy with the trolley – he approached the Kosovars' residence after the fashion of an aged Hamlet mourning the death of Yorick.

The Yorkshire Terrier, the vintage telephone, the clock and the classic guitar were all peddled by Idriz to an antique dealer on the high road, a shaggy, bristly, hoary chap who lurked in the shadows of heavy mahogany wardrobes and Chinese folding screens decorated with gold tone landscapes, red-crowned cranes in bamboo oases, country folk at work and convivial scenes. Idriz squeezed forty pounds out of the antiquarian, after much haggling and straining of his vocal cords. He reinvested the sum pretty damn quick, buying an eighteen-inch sterling silver curb chain, gangsta style, from the pawnbroker next to the Lloyds Bank. The Spalding racket was put to good use by Adelina, who handled it wisely, in the backyard, to beat the dust out of mattresses and duvets, flaunting a disconcerting array of forehands and backhands, with the occasional volley thrown in for good measure. The ashtray and the skull landed on Uncle Tariq's bedside table, both were cherished as poignant memento mori, until at last the skull was fetched, while the old geezer was out and about, by Idriz and Artan's boys, and reclaimed as makeshift football. Of course the kicks it had to endure contributed to make its gaunt grimace even ghastlier.

Ritchie's left foot pain meanwhile, had become so excruciating that he was forced to purchase a pair of adjustable forearm crutches. He saw them on the catalogue of an online dealer, at twenty-five pounds ninety-nine. 'These crutches will get you back on the move after a bone break or a strain.' Read the promotional blurb. 'The tip of the crutch aligns with the hand and shoulder to give you more balance and reduce the fatigue in the hand and wrist. The bottom of the crutches are equipped with slip-resistant rubber tips, to help you gain confidence.'

'Smashing!' Ritchie gasped, and clicking on the buy it now button finalised the transaction.

The Buddha of Queen's Park made quite a splash when, days later, he tottered into Kilburn jobcentre on his spanking new crutches. Walking implements were not a novelty here, at least twenty percent of the employees taking care of the jobseekers in fact ambled on sticks, crutches, or were affected by foot and leg complications, and had to resort to wearing orthopaedic shoes, even to addressing their varicosity problem in the lower extremities by going through some form of exercise, in situ, simply strolling leisurely around the office, limbering up, instead of dealing with petty unemployment matters by staring at their computer desks.

Having been asked to wait at the reception, Ritchie bore patiently his sufferings, trustingly, fully confident that the cathartic power of his affliction would cast him miles ahead on the path of enlightenment. His face was pasty, his eyes had a pitiful, longing expression, he looked like a wiry, twisted trunk, drained of all energy and vital fluids.

At length somebody noticed him, a black lady came toward him puffing and panting, her hair collected in a bun at the back of her head, her blouse and dark,

144

unbuttoned cardigan, loosely wrapped and flapping around the wobbling mass of her weight.

'Do you have a sick note?' she said, ogling the piece of paper Ritchie waved under her nose.

'Yes, I have.'

'But you are in the wrong place,' the receptionist broke in, having read the address of the GP who had issued the certificate. 'You should be signing on at Willesden Green jobcentre, not here!'

'Well, as a matter of fact I have been signing on here for years,' he said.

'That's unusual. Anyway, please write down on this form a brief description of your illness, your full address and telephone number. That's all.'

'How about the work experience? I was due to start next week,' he pressed on.

'That will have to be rearranged. You are not attending it right now!'

Ritchie filled and signed the form, his right elbow propped on the handle of his crutch, then, abandoning pen and paper on the desktop, he clenched both grips and warily made his hobbling exit.

Doctor Rajagopal prescribed Ritchie an X-ray. He bussed his way to the Central Middlesex Hospital, crutched through the hallway and into the radiography wing, waited for the receptionist to show up – a sign on her desk instructed patients to place their prescriptions in a wire mesh tray and take a seat in her absence – she eventually popped out of a back room, a fifty-something, greying blonde lady in a white smock.

'You can just give me your paper, now that I am here,' she sang.

Within minutes a door opened, and a nurse in head scarf with henna tattoos inked all over the right hand and forearm called his name.

'Mr. Richard Barker!'

He got up and swung on his sticks toward her. Once in she told him to take off his left shoe and sock and, sitting on the examination bed placed under the machine, to position the foot over a square slab for the radiogram to be taken.

'Could you move your foot sideways now?' she asked him after a while, coaxingly.

When the second image also had been successfully recorded, the nurse said it was all done. He slipped his sock and shoe on, grabbed the crutches and off he went, back to the hallway and to the bus stop right outside the building.

A couple of days later Sheila too, bewilderingly, turned up with her right foot cast into a brace.

146

'What happened to you?' Ritchie said, looking down at the pearl-grey orthosis and at her toes and nails curiously bared.

'I fell, while on the bus, and injured my ankle,' she explained.

'That's incredible!' he commented, 'I knew travelling on buses could be risky, but it never even crossed my mind that it could be so dangerous.'

She took off her coat, a double-breasted, fuchsia, fashionable little thing. He couldn't help noticing it was new, as she hung it neatly on the pegs in the passage. Her blue skirt must be new as well.

'I see you have been shopping,' he hinted.

'Yes, I have. Since I am not paying any rent I have much more cash to spend on clothes and perfumes,' she owned. 'And then I had to rebuild my wardrobe. My stuff is still being held at auntie's place.'

Ritchie shook his head in disbelief, then treaded softly to the kitchen, dug up two wine glasses out of a cupboard and a bottle of Nero d'Avola from the lower units, poured the wine and made his triumphal entrance into the lounge with the brimming full vessels.

'A toast is needed,' he implied, supporting his enthusiasm with a grinning smile.

'To what?'

'To the new clothes, and to the newfound prosperity!'

'Prosperity my ass, Ritch!' She grumbled. 'I have had to babysit two spoiled brats for hours on end to buy these clothes.'

'Got another job?' He put in.

She had pretty much a new job every single time they met. Her resources were inexhaustible.

'And what did you play at with the boys?'

'They were a boy and a girl. The usual things, board games, doing art, colouring.'

'Smashing!' he said. 'So they must have done your head in.'

'A bit yes, but I get paid for it, so I guess it's okay.'

'Mmm,' he mumbled, the idea of Sheila at play stirred him up, plus he had never engaged in adult games with a crippled person. The foot brace presented to him new challenges, he took to visualise, as she spoke, how many sexual positions or fantasies could be brought into effect by a couple of ailing buddies like themselves.

'I have a business proposition for you,' she burst out instead, which had on his pricked-up senses the same impact a whole bucket of ice cubes emptied over him would have had. 'I happen to know some rich Filipino people,' she went on, 'and they give me commissions, every now and then. They know I am not well-off, so, basically they give me errands, and once I have fulfilled my duties they tip me, so to speak.'

'Sounds interesting,' Ritchie said, hesitantly.

'I was introduced to them by Rodney. He is the one that does all the networking.'

'Didn't you said he was suicidal?'

'He was. He is actually, and will always be, he's been suicidal for most of his adult life, but that doesn't stop him from developing social contacts.'

'Who are these Filipino people then?' Ritchie probed.

'They are a family of restaurateurs. They are planning to open a chain of restaurants here in London, McDonald's style, only slightly posher.'

'Wow, they must be loaded then.'

'They are. Look, to cut the long story short, they asked me a favour, if I could go to Heathrow, next week, and pick up some suitcases for them, as they are too busy to do it themselves apparently.'

'Suitcases? Heathrow? Uhm, it should be easy!'

'Indeed. All I have to do is pick them up, they'll be flying in from Manila, and take them to Hampstead, to their house.'

'Easy peasy.'

'Yup, and they'll reward me with three hundred plodding pounds! What do you think about that?'

'I think it's good!'

'The problem is, I don't have a car, you see?'

'That could be easily sorted,' Ritchie said, 'I believe I could find a car for you, for next week.'

'If you could do that we would share the prize Ritch! One hundred fifty quid each, for two hours' work, how does that sound?'

'Good. Honest work indeed!'

'Will you take me to Heathrow then?'

'How about my own injured foot? I wonder if I will be able to drive at all.'

'Is it the left foot, right?'

'Yes, it is.'

'Does it hurt so much that you can't press it down on the clutch?'

'Not really.'

'Well, then...'

'Okay, I will,' he clinched. 'Consider it done!'

In the evening he called mum, his very own, personal troubleshooter.

'How is Josh then?' He inquired with much solicitude.

'The staphylococcus is not causing any more trouble right now, although it is still there. The hernia is not in the final stages, but neither is receding. He must bear his cross with patience.'

'Yeah, I suppose so. Valery must be much worried, I guess.'

'She looked up over the internet for natural remedies to fever and flu, as he is always unwell. She found out, for example, that ginger keeps fever away, and started mixing it, in powder, into his tea, in the morning.'

'That's clever!' He said.

'How about you, is your foot being very troublesome?'

'Just a wee bit. Yes, it burns inside, I am currently on crutches.'

'Was it that bad?'

'I bought the crutches to keep it off the ground for a while, until it gets better, that's all.'

'Let's hope it works. Your father has been diagnosed with cataracts, he will have to go under the knife.'

'No way! When?'

'It could take months, there is a long queue ahead of him, surely before the end of the year though.'

'I'll keep fingers crossed mum. Hey listen, I wanted to ask, is it going to be okay if I borrow the car? Next Wednesday? Only for a few hours.'

'We haven't got anything planned for Wednesday, so it should be okay Ritch.'

'Is it okay if I come around on Tuesday evening? I'll bring the car back by Wednesday lunchtime.'

'All right, I'll check with dad, but there should be no problems.'

'Will there be fuel in the car?'

'There should be. I can't guarantee it a hundred per cent.'

'Okay, thanks mum, I love you,' Ritchie said. 'And dad, too!'

The grand cashed in by Artan on occasion of the Grand National had a reinvigorating effect on him, he behaved with newly acquired self-assurance, at the office, betting very little, surveying the proceedings in a detached, debonair attitude instead, tipping off fellow luck chasers from the vertiginous height of the winning pedestal on which he had wondrously been raised. However quickly, or ineffectually the money would be spent, the glow of the winner's aura lighting him up – a supernatural glow, almost – would be refulgently undeniable, it was not going to be wiped off easily, just as well as a hard-to-beat record set by a true champion, his feat would be remembered in living memory.

Another benefit of the winning coup was of course the liberality of banqueting and feasting it had introduced in the Kosovars' retreat. Succulent roasted meats besieged by swarms of oven-hot, sizzling, golden tanned potato wedges graced their table even on the blandest of weekdays. He purchased patent leather black shoes to match his festive outfit, giving them such a thorough shine they could be used as a mirror to make sure his well-oiled haircut was tidily side-parted. His kids were gifted a much thirsted for video game console – until now only caught glimpses of in studiedly cheerful TV ads – his wife, Tereza, was presented with a gold chain bracelet, a pre-owned one, that jingled and clinked to the merry melody of the several charms dangling from it, among which a twisted, lucky horn featured glaringly, meant to channel good fortune in their direction even more abundantly.

As for Ritchie, his weekend, for a change, was a contemplative one, spent looking after his spiritual gifts, re-energising and recharging his batteries in the peaceful, soothing atmosphere of his private sanctuary. Strangely enough, there were no messages from Lady Davina, or anybody else so far. He was forced to admit that no matter how popular an awakened one might be, a pause in the intensity of his relations could just be around the corner, independently from his ardent desire to be hugely and constantly in demand. 'When nobody calls you,' he pondered, 'there's nothing you can do but sit and wait. Until a new wave of devotion will make you soar once again on the wings of Buddhahood.'

Sheila spent the weekend dreaming of the suitcases, of what their contents might be. They would be jetted all the way around the world, from sunny Manila, her hometown, bringing with them a whiff of the tropics, hints of the paradise lost that Philippines had become for her after all these years of Northern European colourless indifference. Her vision was pushed even further, along the tracks of glorious new beginnings, and the suitcases suddenly opened up, by magic, to show layers of banknotes neatly stacked and ready to be grabbed, pocketed, squandered in the West End from one fancy shop to the next, in an unprecedented spree, a splurge of such consequences that the evening papers would have had to mention it regardless of her non-existence on the London VIP scene.

On Tuesday evening, as agreed, Ritchie rode the tube to Stanmore. It was drizzly, one of those closes of the day characterised by an overwhelming excess of dampness in the air. Raindrops were so subtle they came across as a widespread spray against the luminous circles irradiated by the streetlights. Their random bouncing off could have been compared to molecular activity seen through the microscope. As a result, when he came out of the station, the fifteen-minute stretch of road to his parents' house felt like a swinging stroll on crutches in a giant bubble of soapy water, the boundaries between dry and wet having been totally swallowed up in the fine-grained washout.

Janet Barker answered the door in woolly jumper, slacks and slippers. She gave him a pitying look. Ritchie broke into a reassuring smile and limped in. He found dad at the desk, in the room that had once been his very own, busy on the computer with crossword puzzles.

'Hey Ritch!' he said, 'how is life treating you?'

'Poorly dad. No job, no money, no girlfriend, and a faulty foot!'

'That's too bad,' the old man said, peering at him over the reading glasses. 'But it's understandable, these are difficult times we are going through, companies do not hire people indefinitely, as when your mother and I were young. As for the foot, it will get better soon, trust me.'

'You must never lose hope,' mum chimed in. 'Sooner or later your big break will come.'

'Yeah, before retirement, hopefully,' Ritchie quipped.

In less than half an hour he snatched the car keys from the wall hanger by the main door, let mum and dad hug and kiss him as he held on tight to his sticks, and was off in their white Nissan. Once in the driver's seat he tossed his crutches at the back, performed a few rotatory exercises with the ailing extremity, and then went on pressing down the clutch with it. It felt quite all right, the source of the pain must be somewhere in the ligaments, or even deeper, in the bones, and the prove of it was that setting the foot down didn't make things any worse. He fastened the seat belt, turned the key in, and started the car.

The drive home revived memories of practical tests and nervy evening lessons, years ago, when he had been much keener on the prospect of swerving through the traffic on four wheels. His driving licence, though, had acquired, in time, the status of an additional ID card, winding up in his wallet to gather mould and dust as, partly for his work precarity, partly for his off-the-scale indolence, he had never really been promoted to proficiency as a motorist, but rather remained in a greyish limbo populated by the lost souls of all other fledgling drivers and bunglers alike.

He parked the car on the other side of the road for the night, not far from the patchy trunk of one of the plane trees branching out in the avenue, hopped back in his flat, hooked up the crutches on the pegs in the passage, dropped the two sets of keys on the coffee table and slumped heavily on the sofa, to indulge in a speculative sneak preview of what was required of him the following day.

Then, almost by association with the cucumber coolness that pervaded him – something that tended to take place, invariably, as the small hours drew near – he focused on tranquil abiding, one of the virtuous objects of meditation, number nineteen for the precision, in the list of twenty-one delineated in lamrim, the textual font presenting the stages of the path to enlightenment as taught by Buddha. Tranquil abiding was indeed what appealed most to him when the hustle and bustle of worldly preoccupations ceased to exert its pressure on his high-flying spirit.

'O Blessed One,' he cried, 'Shakyamuni Buddha, precious treasury of compassion, bestower of supreme inner peace, you, who love all beings without exception, are the source of happiness and goodness, and you guide us to the liberating path.'

The morning after, Sheila came around shortly past nine. She wore a puffy pair of blue shorts over black stockings – a 'forced choice,' in her own words, to allow room for the foot brace – and a silky black blouse and blazer.

'Wow! You're dressed to impress,' Ritchie said.

'I wanted to look professional,' she replied, 'despite the injury.'

'I shall wear a jacket, too!' He added, and disappeared past the bedroom door, re-emerging in a minute or two in white shirt and black, casual blazer. Having smoothed down his hair with his hands in the mirror hung above the sofa, he picked up the two sets of keys from the coffee table and unhooked the inseparable crutches from the coat rack, then they both gimped downstairs. Ritchie, however, was in for a shocking surprise, as soon as they were out in the street he gaped dumbfoundedly at his parents' formerly white Nissan maculated with splotches of birds' droppings from headlights to boot.

'Oh, my God!' He uttered in disbelief.

The car had been severely whipped by a torrent of yolky, creamy-white splutters, now hardened into crusty blotches. A storm of avian excrement had been lashing out at it.

'We're going to look very shitty!' Ritchie couldn't help muttering, taking a contemptuous look at the thick canopy of branches, high up, where the culprits must have been lodged overnight, and where their discharges must have cascaded from.

Anyway, there was no time to wash the car. They must be going, he would have had to do it later on.

They jumped in. He switched on the on-board computer and selected the destination: Heathrow, Terminal 4, seventeen miles, forty-one minutes away, turn left in a hundred ten yards, and left again in a hundred ninety, then right on to Dudden Hill Lane, zero point five miles later.

'Smashing!' Ritchie groaned, starting the car and following blindly the sat-nav orbital directions. 'Hey, listen, I wanted to ask you, do you actually know what's in these suitcases we are going to pick up?'

'Nope.' Sheila said bluntly. 'To be honest with you I have been wondering myself what there might be in them, but I have no clue. I suppose they must be full of personal effects.'

'Yeah, I guess so.' He went on dreamily. 'So they are so rich they don't even have time to collect their luggage?'

'Yes, they are.'

On the North Circular Road he took to cruise at moderate speed on the slow lane, not to strain his convalescent left foot, also to keep a low profile after months, perhaps years of absence from London's main traffic arteries. The last thing he wanted was to bring the car back with a scratch or, even worse, a dent. As he had done once, in foolhardier days, having skidded on the wet motorway against the guardrail, in a sharp curve, shattering the main headlight on the driver's side and scraping part of the bodywork of an older Vauxhall tremendously dear to his dad. The accident had sparked a 4:00 a.m. heated squabble in his parents' bedroom, with both of them shouting and snarling at him, making him feel as guilty and flushed out as a proper offender, colouring his misdeed with tinges that were nothing short of criminal. Surely he didn't want to go back there.

By the time they had reached the M4 Sheila resumed her frisky moods, which were quite an out-of-the-blue occurrence given the absence of wine – he had always firmly believed the intensity boosts to her playfulness were directly proportional to the quantity of red wine she had been quaffing – she stretched her right hand in a cursory fashion on to his left thigh, stroking it with friendly intentions at first, then with increasing sensuousness, much more invitingly. Soon it was clear she was aiming to set a reaction in motion, to stir in him sensations not exactly pertinent to the road or driving, or to their leisurely undertaking. And eventually she succeeded in doing so, Ritchie's crotch bulged visibly. Sheila unzipped his fly, slipped the lecherous hand in the burrow, confident that she was going to pluck the rabbit by its ears, or a twitchy snake more like. Seconds later she went down on him, minding not to bury the gear knob under the mild arch of her wriggling torso.

When they were half a mile away from Terminal 4 a massive cargo aircraft swooped down thunderingly over their heads.

'Hey, those could be our suitcases up there, we should hurry up,' Ritchie said.

'I couldn't make out if it were a Philippine Airlines plane, but you might be right,' Sheila conceded.

The glass facade of the flat, elongated building, suddenly loomed on their left hand-side, the limitless sky and its banks of clouds projected on it as though on the widest screen ever conceived. All they had to do now was park the befouled car. A couple of escalators later Ritchie and Sheila made their orthopaedically challenged appearance in the airport lounge. The hall was milling with passengers shooting in all directions, some lugging handy suitcases on wheels, some others pushing larger trolleys loaded with bulkier travelling bags. The clinking and scraping of cutlery against saucers and plates echoed under the lofty ceiling as they coasted the numerous bars and food outlets giving out a fragrant scent of coffee, baked rolls and sizzling crispy bacon.

Ritchie's businesslike mindset did not admit of digressions in such a momentous confluence. He was so taken by the perspective of carrying out this operation swiftly and successfully that the whole carousel of lights and colours whirling around him amounted to nothing, had no hold on him. Finally, he spotted the baggage reclaim banana-yellow sign and pointed at it with the half-raised tip of his left crutch. Sheila was mesmerised by the sight of the neon-lit rectangle, for an instant she was genuinely awestruck. At last they thought wise to follow the arrow.

Sheila checked one more time the ticket she had been given by her employers, bearing the numbers of the five, black, identical suitcases she would have to collect.

'The flight from Manila will be unloaded in bay number eight,' Ritchie told her after he'd scanned the arrivals board.

There was the usual melee at the conveyor belt merry-go-round, those in the second or third row jostling their way to the front as soon as something vaguely resembling what they thought was theirs was glimpsed. Sheila lumbered up to a docking station to free a four-wheeler from a line of baggage trolleys.

About ten minutes later five, identical, black suitcases with five numbered red paper ribbons wrapped around the handles popped up on the carousel.

'Those must be ours!' Sheila said, flapping her ticket under Ritchie's nose.

They both sidled up to the conveyor belt, and clumsily managed to pull the suitcases down, dragging them on to the trolley. Ritchie had to lay down the crutches for a while to use his hands, whereas Sheila complained, shortly afterwards, about a new surge of pain in her sprained ankle. Having secured their precious freight, Ritchie and Sheila staggered through the Customs red portal, and on to the very end of the antiseptically white corridor leading to the area designed for inspections. Two officers in white shirts and black jumpers then helped them to ease the suitcases up on a counter.

'Anything to declare?' asked the senior officer, a balding guy with a greyish-blue stubble smuggled for a beard and a riled, stern expression.

'These are not our suitcases!' Sheila remonstrated. 'We're only running an errand on behalf of friends.'

All of a sudden an English Foxhound was released, from a back door, and burst wagging his tail on to the scene.

'Go on George,' spurred the stubbly guy. 'Go on, good boy!'

George's moist and shiny rhinarium was all tingly, he must have sniffed out something so powerfully smelly it was driving his olfactory system crazy. His alertness was such as only the spoor of a wild animal could have triggered.

'We must open these suitcases!' The officer announced.

'Help yourselves,' Sheila said.

Immediately, as the stubbly guy flipped up the drawbolt catches of the first suitcase, George had to be held back, his excitement could barely be contained, he sprang up on his hind legs, even as the younger officer – a dark-haired, plumper, spectacled bloke – pulled funny faces, bound as he was not to let go of the harness. The red ribbon was rent, then the stubbly officer flung the suitcase open.

'Uhm, let's see what we've got here,' he said thoughtfully.

There was nothing remotely similar to personal effects inside, as Sheila had imagined, but neatly packaged, white blocks instead. For a handful of panicky seconds Ritchie feared the worst. He was led to believe there might be some illegal substances in those white parcels. The officer went on picking one of the packets, gauged it summarily, it felt like a quarter of meat, a beef joint, tightly wrapped in butcher's greaseproof paper. He slid a pocketknife in the fold where the sheet ends overlapped and went on cutting the wraps. A ruby-red, dried-up chunk of flesh enveloped in airtight, clear plastic film, was duly exposed, so that everyone may witness the violation.

'Well, well, well,' he bawled. 'Houston, we have a problem! Under present regulations,' he proceeded to state, 'all meat products from outside EU must be declared in advance, it is an offence to import meat and poultry from other continents, unless they be thoroughly tested and given the okay.'

'We were kept in the dark as to the contents of the suitcases!' Sheila protested.

'Penalties for such transgressions may vary,' the officer, inflexible, insisted, 'from fines of up to five thousand pounds, to two years in jail.'

'We are absolutely innocent!' Ritchie joined in while the tiniest, beady sweat drops surfaced on his forehead, temples and brows.

It turned out the suitcases were chock-full of pork, lamb, beef and goat consignments, plus a few more helpings of so-called bushmeat – the meat of animals roaming free in the wild, such as monkeys, elephants, and oriental sausages of undefined provenience (they might just as well have been made out of cats and dogs) – imported for the speciality ethnic markets. There were also fish and cheeses, in two of the five suitcases, but those could get through customs all right, as long as they didn't exceed twenty kilos, which fortunately they didn't, in this specific case.

After much pleading and begging, and new assertions meant to clarify this hot stuff was not their property after all, and that they had been the hapless victims of a vicious stitch-up, Ritchie and Sheila had to consider themselves lucky that customs officers had opted to seize the illegal imports and impose no other sanctions on them. Yet the suitcases felt worryingly light, as they loaded them again on to the trolley and found their way down to the car park.

'This doesn't look good, Ritch!' Sheila warned when they were back in the car. 'The Fernandez family will be much pissed off, collectively, and I am afraid I'll be in for an ear-straining bollocking.'

'It's not my problem, darling,' he said. 'I am gonna drop you and your suitcases in Hampstead, then you'll deal with them. I did my bit.'

'Thanks a lot, Ritch! What if they are not going to pay me?'

'If they won't pay you, I guess you should give me something to make up for the trouble caused. I was nearly fainting when the chap unwrapped that joint of meat. I might have easily had a heart attack!'

'But you didn't have it, you made it through customs just fine. Anyway, they should tip me all the same, I have brought them their damn suitcases, even though half-empty.'

Ritchie pulled over in Keats' Grove, in front of the gate of a white stucco Georgian house, a box-shaped, compact building with a semi-circular balcony jutting out of the facade and a fancy, tiled canopy on spindly columns above the main door.

'Good luck!' he said, once he had helped her unload the suitcases and lined them up on the kerb. 'I am off, got things to do, cheerio!'

Sheila rang the bell. Ritchie hopped in dad's white Nissan and drove on. On his way home he had some time to himself to go over the facts of the day. What had taken place was a further confirmation, if there was still need of one, of the incongruity and futility of active life, especially when compared to the sublime heights only the spirit and an enlightened mind could attain through contemplation. He had been tempted once again to resume his old ways, and the preposterousness of the entire episode was the quashing evidence, proving once and for all that he didn't belong to such lowly spheres, mundane cares were not meant for him, he'd better stick to the choice of wisdom as the sole ruler of his life, rather than give in to these raids into the unpredictable domain of earthly tribulations. Never again he'd be stooping so low, be dragged down in the mud where only imperfect beings wallow and thrive. His soul was made to soar.

He parked the car again on the other side of the road, a couple of yards away from a drain, swung across the driving lanes on his crutches, climbed the three steps to the door, and slipped in. Minutes later he reappeared in shirtsleeves, aided by one crutch only, propped up against his left elbow, a pail full of hot soapy water in his right hand, on the bubbly surface an old bath sponge floated like a bark in a storm out at sea. He set the bucket down next to the car, gave the sponge a good soaking, then went on scrubbing off all the bird poo encrusted on the roof and bonnet, minding not to neglect the dried-up streaks of what had dripped alongside the flanks of the vehicle. When he had almost done, a police car meandered cautiously toward him, coming up from the high road. The last thing on his mind was they would be after him, but surprisingly they were. The car stopped flush with dad's Nissan and three officers in white shirts and stab proof vests got off.

'Good morning, sir!' Hailed a stout fellow with a grey stubble of cropped hair covering his pate and piercing blue eyes.

'Good morning,' Ritchie answered. 'Is there anything wrong?'

The other two policemen, a younger chap and a middle-aged one of Asian origins, were weighing the slow but steady, trickling flow of suds into the drain.

'Sir, it is environmentally unsafe to let chemical discharges, such as those caused by detergents, run off into the sewage system,' the blue-eyed cop rebuked. 'There is a fine for that!' He added, and producing a pre-stamped sheet scribbled down on it the particulars of the incident, plus eighty pounds in legible digits, signed it and handed it over. 'Here's a penalty notice,' he said, 'with an eighty pound fine. You have twenty-eight days to appeal to a court of justice or to pay the fine, whichever comes easier. Good day, sir!'

'Grim news Ritch!' Sheila shouted down the receiver.

'What's up?' Ritchie said.

'They only gave me a hundred quid!'

'No way!'

'They said more than half their goods were gone, they said we ought to have gone straight through the blue or green gate, not the red one, nobody would have stopped us.'

'I see, it's our fault then.'

'Yup. We still get fifty pounds each,' she said reassuringly.

She couldn't have known that with the eighty pound fine snatched up on the exit from their airport adventure the balance was thirty quid down for him.

On a positive note, on Thursday morning, Nop texted him, asking if he wanted to take her out, nothing fancy, just a spot of shopping down Portobello Road.

'Okay,' he replied, 'what time shall we meet?'

'Let's do earlier, at four?'

'Fine, see you at four in Notting Hill Gate then?'

'Yes.' She typed.

He was much aggrieved by the events of the last twenty-four hours, also, it had rarely happened that he had been on more than two dates with the same person without any profitable outcome. This was Nop's last chance to shine. If nothing would come of it he'd be looking forward to move on.

She was cussedly late, as usual. Nonetheless coming out of the station, she sauntered insouciantly toward him in her grey, cowgirl boots, just as though time mattered very little to her. The first shop she dragged him into was the chemist wedged between the houseware store and the phone service provider. Nop took to inspect one by one beauty products displayed on shelves running the whole length of a long aisle. Ritchie was irresistibly attracted to the reading glasses stand. He tried on a pair with rectangular, purplish frames, and peered at his phone through the lenses to have a general idea of their focusing correction power, then swapped it with a plus one diopter pair, and again made sure the lenses didn't strain his eyes. By the time he had found the eyewear that suited him – he had to fuss back and forth with the plus one diopter, plus one point five and plus two in order to establish that – as well as determined he was not going to buy any of it, Nop was queuing at the till, a hair lotion in one hand and the tan wallet with her bank card peeping out of one leathery pocket in the other.

They marched down Portobello Road as agreed, but moods were sulky. The warm exchanges of their first meeting had dwindled to the odd complimentary enunciation thrown in by Ritchie to fill a gap, an evident absence of content, chemistry, and common ground. She said she wanted to go to the pound shop. He pointed in the right direction and showed the way. Again, the Thai girl perused products and scanned shelves with painstaking accuracy. Ritchie followed her one or two paces back, observing her with detachment, the flummoxed expression elicited by a work of art allowing for discordant interpretations freezing his face. She purchased a family pack of crisps, a can of tuna in sunflower oil, tampons and wipes.

'Done,' she said when past the glass doors and out on the pavement, 'I don't need to buy anything else!'

He nodded and pointed the way once more, perfunctorily, rather lost for words. Quite simply he couldn't believe she had lured him out of his den to buy crisps, tuna and hair dye, or whatever was in the box she had picked up at the chemist. He moped in silence as they retraced their steps to the station. In Notting Hill Gate she said she was going to get the bus instead of the tube, so he waited with her at the bus stop. Minutes went awkwardly and speechlessly by, then the double decker sailed in. He gave her one last look, raised his left hand, and waved her goodbye. Nop loped on to the platform and was swallowed by the press of standing passengers, the doors closed and the driver steered on.

Only the comfort of prayer – more mantras were faithfully recited right after dusk had stretched its appeasing shadows in the sky – and of a large glass of Pinot Noir, with its vibrant array of red fruit aromatics meant to deliver a resilient finish across the palate – along these lines the online reviews hyped it up – could restore Ritchie's equanimity.

On Friday morning, long after the breakfast ritual and the daily ablutions had been carried out, an unexpected phone call broke the monotony of his idle hours.

'Hello, Mr. Barker?'

'Yes, it is I, erm... Me. Him.' Ritchie bumbled.

'I am calling from your bank, just to inform you that we have conducted the appropriate investigations, and having found no foul play so far decided to reactivate your card.'

'Thank you so much,' he said.

'We apologise for any inconvenience caused. If you like, I could enrol you, free of charge, in a programme that aims to prevent fraud.'

'Free of charge?' He spelled out the magic words.

'Absolutely. What is going to happen is, any time an unusual transaction will show on your account, the bank will call you to ensure it is really you who are giving the okay for it.'

'Smashing! Go ahead, please.'

'You'll receive a letter with the details. Bye now.'

'Thanks. Bye.'

No sooner had he hung up than a spontaneous invocation resonated in his relieved mind: 'oh Buddha, oh Buddha, may my card make me well, happy and peaceful.'

Later on, inexorable, Lady Davina's latest message was delivered: 'I hope you are feeling better? I assume you have been too unwell to call me?'

He reckoned he wasn't ill to the point of being unable to meet her for a drink. His reply was therefore auspicious, encouraging too, to a mild extent. 'I am feeling better indeed,' he wrote, although it wasn't exactly true – his foot injury was far from full recovery, and worse still, the causes of those burning, knifing fits hadn't been established yet – 'how have you been?'

Perplexingly though, his cheerful attempt to bridge the gap distance had opened between the lady and himself, fell like a fruitless drop in the proverbial ocean of mobile communication. His message didn't even seem to have reached its target, or else Lady Davina, with these brief notes of hers, had gradually undergone a baffling transformation, from a flesh and blood being to a ghostly presence inhabiting the microprocessors of digital devices. Where was she texting from? It was hard to fathom. Canada? Australia? From the Galapagos, Greenland, or from the Kamchatka Peninsula? She might as well be addressing him from Cape Horn as far as Ritchie was concerned.

The next appointment with Doctor Rajagopal would be decisive in terms of throwing new light on the shortcomings of his left foot. He popped in the surgery on Wednesday morning, as early as the glass door of the Medical Centre rolled on its sliding track and, having queued his way to the reception, was given an audience with the GP in little more than a couple of hours' time, before lunchtime.

Rajagopal, in blue and white floral dress, arched her eyebrows when he hopped in on crutches. Ritchie sat down beside the desk and, laying the walking sticks down across his lap, readied to hear the verdict.

'The X-ray shows there is nothing wrong with the bone structure of your foot,' she announced. 'In my opinion this is a case of severe inflammation of the epithelial tissue.'

Ritchie nodded attentively. 'Is there a solution for that?' he asked.

'I will prescribe some tablets, to help you deal with the pain, and a gel, to give the foot a gentle rubbing. Let's see how things go, if there will be any improvement.'

Rajagopal kept staring at the computer screen, as though the answers to the wide range of afflictions brought daily to her attention would miraculously flash, any moment now, right before her eyes, like a divine decree entrusted to the cold codifications of the machine.

'Thank you very much, doctor,' Ritchie said, accompanying words with the slightest bow of his head.

'Come to see us in a couple of weeks to let us know if you are feeling any better.'

'I will,' he granted, and getting back on his sticks, wobbled out of the office.

On his way home Ritchie witnessed a modest, downcast crowd gathered not far off the high road. It was more like a cluster of neighbours loitering in the front yard of one of the terraced houses whereas, on the other side of the road, Idriz, Edonis, Uncle Tariq and Grandpa Andri, arms folded, leaned their back against the rusting wrought iron and red brick fence hemming in their council retreat and kept watch on the proceedings.

On the first floor of the house besieged by the loiterers, in a dingy mahogany bedroom that had seen better days, on a four poster bed that had lost its shine long ago, Mrs. Jones had been laid out in her pale blue colonial nightgown with scalloped collar over paisley lace embroideries. Without the glasses, once rigor mortis had set in, her profile looked inflexibly austere, all the chirpy cheerfulness she had always been known for had deserted her.

There was no need of pomp or pallbearers, when the wake was over, to get her out of the house. She had shrunk to a mere sack of bones, and two funeral directors in black livery and top hat were more than enough to carry the coffin downstairs and heave it on to the Cadillac, where a white daisy wreath angled against a window spelled MUM. Only three cars trailed behind the procession, Mrs. Jones' daughter, Laura, with her husband and two teenage boys, trundled immediately after the hearse, in the other two vehicles an assortment of distant relatives had been conjured up at the last minute. It could be said the deceased was more popular among neighbours than with what was left of her family.

The funeral service was held in St. Andrew's Parish Church, under the merciful eye of a realistic statue of the Sacred Heart of Jesus.

'The Lord is my shepherd;' read father Michael Bambridge once the coffin had been laid before the altar. 'I lack nothing. He makes me lie down in green pastures and leads me beside still waters. He shall refresh my soul and guide me in the paths of righteousness for his name's sake. Even though I walk through the valley of the shadow of death, I will fear no evil; for you are with me...'

Laura's cheeks were streaked with warm tears, yet she felt way too dejected to wipe them out, the tender love for her mother, and the knowledge that, in this life, she would meet her no more, had uncorked a cataract of despairing sensations.

The final stage of the ceremony was enacted in the Willesden New Cemetery, where Mrs. Jones was laid to rest only a few feet apart from her husband, Robert, prompting in the mourners the somewhat comforting thought that, despite all, the couple had been reunited at last.

Uncle Tariq had smoked with gusto while the coffin had been carried out of the front door and secured at the back of the Cadillac. When the majority of onlookers had made the sign of the cross, he had turned his face aside and spat contemptuously on the pavement. Idriz had managed, on the other hand, to keep his composure, he might even have been touched by the sudden departure, judging from his dour demeanour. He had fidgeted with his sterling silver necklace, bitten and chewed on it, as the procession was set in motion, but given no signs of impatience. Grandpa Andri had cleared his throat, groaned, poised his lips as if something worth paying attention to would come out of them, and uttered no other sounds instead. Adelina had stood back, monitoring activities from her hiding nook, behind the glass pane of the living room window, hardly moved by the collective display of sorrow.

Two days after the burial of Mrs. Jones, on a sunny and relatively warm afternoon, the Bosnia and Herzegovina Community Centre Advice, much to Idriz and the gang's elation, reopened its doors to the public. Tea and biscuits were served, as senior refugees and younger alike tottered in to find again a corner of their homeland safely preserved in the heart of the borough, and an inaugural speech was given by the president of the club, a septuagenarian, plump gent with a well-trimmed white beard and a tweed jacket over olive-green trousers, whose eyes seemed to be the living testament of the horrors experienced during the three years eight months one week and six days the conflict had raged on.

'We will hopefully be able,' Mr. Hasi said from his pulpit, 'from now on, to enjoy a peaceful stay in this country, and I take this opportunity to say thank you to the local MP, Miss Lara Thermot, for the kindly support she has offered us in times of distress.'

A big round of applause from all sections of the audience raised the club's newly mended roof, then there were more refreshments, and more congratulations going all around the room.

Hours later, just as fluffs of pink clouds stretched to the horizon, and the temporary gilding of Wembley arch shot high up over the roofs, in the distance, gleaming on account of the last darts of brightness fired against it by the setting sun, Edonis and his girlfriend, Gentiana, were the first guests to wind up at Idriz's place. Idriz's and Artan's boys were squatting in the front yard, flicking marbles against the red-brick lower half of the fence, Uncle Tariq did the honours, slipping a can of lager into Edonis' gripping right hand and showing his girlfriend the way to the kitchen, where she would be likely to join

Adelina for a catch-up on the latest celebrity gossips. Meanwhile Idriz was warming up his fingers, at the keyboard, and the clunking notes flowed freely out of the living room, as the window had been left wide open – the removal of Mrs. Jones, a fateful turn of events by all means, reduced the chances of neighbours lodging a complaint to an insignificant percentage, therefore, and rather luckily, given the sudden occurrence of the mini heatwave, no fears of letting noises out would blight the party tonight.

Gezim and Mirjeta soon arrived. They parked their violet Ford Capri somewhere down the road and strolled back to the house. She wore a gypsy, long black gown and black top, the jet-black hair collected in a top knot held together with a few bobby pins, and looked truly ravishing. One by one Dritan, Milot, Sokol, Ramiz, Liridon, Saban and Lavdrim all dropped by, and the party was soon in full swing.

'Baby you can drive my car,' sang Idriz, solidly planted centre stage in the soundproofed living room, 'yes I'm gonna be a star, baby you can drive my car, and maybe I'll love you, beep beep'm beep yeah, beep beep'm beep beep yeah...'

The boys and girls, scattered at random in the passage and out in the front yard – only Sokol, Dritan and Edonis sat on the floor facing Idriz and his Yamaha, since temperature in the music room tended to soar quickly, once the keyboard was skilfully fingered – merrily sipped lager from the can and tapped their feet to the tune.

After he had downed three cans of lager and puffed avidly on a dozen fags, Uncle Tariq's morbid sensibility spurred him to embark on a raving eulogy in a sulky, embittered mood. He retrieved his skull from the backyard, where the kids had been kicking it around, and finding it all tatty and toothless, gave it a summary wipe with the cuff of his flannel shirt and, holding it in his left hand, walked back in and down the passage. Milot was the first guest to notice his sharp humour change.

'Hey, Uncle Tariq, what's that skull for? This is a party!' he said.

'A party my ass!' The old geezer groused. 'This is not a party, it's a funeral!'

'Ha ha! What funeral? Nobody is dead.'

'The old bird is dead,' Uncle Tariq sentenced, stroking the chipped, bruised cranium. 'The old bird is dead.'

There was some dancing, too, before midnight, when Idriz switched effortlessly from pop tunes to Balkan folk music. Grandpa Andri and Adelina got the ball rolling, followed by Gezim and Mirjeta – she had to lift her gypsy gown up, above the knees, and hold it with her left hand while her partner made her twirl around with well-timed flicks of his wrist – and by Edonis and Gentiana. Some of the guys formed couples as well, and joined in, pirouetting and chuckling, their bellies gurgling for all the beer they had been chugging.

That night, between one and two, if anybody happened to be hanging around in the little square before the main entrance of the Willesden New Cemetery, he'd have seen a bunch of about a dozen men slightly drunk, although not boisterously so, heading for the burial ground. He'd have then observed with what self-control, like a platoon well-versed in drill and military discipline, said men proceeded to scale the pedestrians' small gate, one of them – Grandpa Andri, for the record – joining hands to provide a footing for the others, and relying on the forearm and hand grip of the last of his comrades to go over the barrier, even though his porcine belly kept him firmly anchored to the ground, despite the energy with which he had been hauled up, and he had no choice but to wait outside. They had to trek for quite a while through hundreds of graves lined up along the paths, in the dewy, grassy beds, often venturing in the unexplored territory of the second, third and fourth rows, where treading grew treacherous by the faint radiance of the crescent moon. It was the freshly dug earth, the unmistakable whiteness of the gravestone and a pot of blooming chrysanthemums to set them on the right tracks and have them assembled over the intended spot at last.

'There was grace in her steps, love in every gesture.
She touched everyone with special love and kindness.
Lost now but loved forever.
For with God nothing shall be impossible.
Here lies Henrietta Jones, 11th February 1937-5th June 2013, beloved mum, reunited with dad.'

Read the headstone inscription. Behind it, on a plinth, the fifty-five-inch statue of a winged, long-haired, androgynous angel holding a lamp in his right hand, while the left was gently placed over his chest, kept vigil on the mortal spoils of Mrs. Jones.

'Here is the old bird!' said Uncle Tariq slurring his words.

Upon which by mutual, unspoken accord, the whole gang formed a semicircle at the foot of the grave and, unzipping their flies, the guys went on exposing their willies to the cool air of the reasonably mild night and peed with much satisfaction on the old lady's new domicile. The parabolic jets of eleven amber fountains irrigated Mrs. Jones' patch, steaming in a quiet corner of the cemetery, the dark shadow of Roundwood Park hill looming in the distance, in the shape of a humongous beached whale about to exhale her last breath.

Their duty absolved, Uncle Tariq, inflamed, in a flashing instant of fancy, lecherously hugged the angel and, leaning heavily against it, took to unroot the statue. The angel swayed under the increasing pressure, gave way, until it finally came loose. Once it had been grounded, with the help of Milot, who cradled the head, the old geezer, handling the plinth, gave directions for the transport of the winged beauty back to their retreat. A good deal of careful manoeuvring was necessary to get it over and past the gate, but twelve pair of arms proved more than enough to ensure the statue safe passage into the world of the living.

'What's next?' wondered Morgan O'Driscoll, on Monday morning, in the succinct headline of his front-page article on the Kilburn Times. 'A wild bunch of non-identified troublemakers has been climbing the gates of the Willesden New Cemetery, last Saturday, in the early hours, sometime between 1:00 and 2:00 a.m. local time, allegedly, to desecrate and vandalise Mrs. Henrietta Jones' resting place. The felony is only the last in a string of scathing attacks on the dead, including previous asportation of bronze plaques from the monument to the fallen of World War II, most probably for lucrative ends, the recycling of marbles and masonry works, and the repeated defiling of corpses. We should ask ourselves: will this spate of sacrilegious acts ever come to an end? And if not, what to expect next?'

As for the angel, with a few trowelfuls of quick drying cement it was planted bang in the middle of the concrete backyard, featuring as an oversized gnome, or any other garden sculpture. However pretty soon Adelina put it to better use, coiling a washing line around its neck and letting it run the whole length of the court, for improved hanging facilities.

On the Buddhist front, the setbacks of the last few weeks had persuaded Ritchie to carry out a scrupulous self-assessment, in order to establish if the path he was treading was indeed the one that would lead him to enlightenment. The impermanence of the universe, and the transmigration of all beings through innumerable existential planes – even heaven, in Buddhism, is only a temporary destination – encouraged him, in this delicate juncture, as never before, to search for that perfect condition that, alone, could guarantee him an all-round, unassailable wellness. How to enter that pure land, how to achieve that mental state that would make him feel solidly rooted down like a prospering, centuries-old tree, rather than being loosely unanchored, like an ever-bending reed caught in the eye of the storm, those were the questions he turned over in his mind.

Days flew by uneventfully, his throbbing and sore left foot was the sole remainder that life and blood were still waxing and waning in him at the usual rhythms, that the pulse was still lending him a new lease of vigour, and would keep doing so for quite a while. Then he realised that nothing better than a good old betting spree would do to rebuild the integrity of his soul. Besides Royal Ascot was on, so how on earth could he have failed to put in an appearance or two at the office? Not showing up would have been perceived as a lack of respect for fellow gamblers, for the entire horse racing confraternity, a global affront. Go he must.

On Tuesday afternoon the Queen Anne Stakes could not be missed for the world. Ritchie and Artan watched with trepidation as the royal procession trundled on the Berkshire course. In her horse-drawn landau, decked out in a peach-coloured dress and hat, the queen was eagerly cheered upon arrival. Regrettably, Prince Philip was not by her side, having been admitted to hospital on the

176

previous Tuesday and having been ordered absolute rest for the time being. Camilla Parker Bowles, in a cream coloured dress and hat and white top, sat in place of the queen's consort. As soon as the procession approached the grandstand, the band of the Scots Guards converged in circle in the Parade Ring and struck up the national anthem. Hats were taken off and respectfully held at half-mast.

'God save our gracious Queen, long live our noble Queen, God save the Queen!' Sang Ritchie on his crutches. 'She is hilarious, happy and gregarious, long to reign over all, God save the Queen!' He went on, making up the lyrics where he didn't remember exactly what they were like.

Artan just stood erect beside him, puffing his chest, mouthing something vague, if only for the sake of being thankful for the asylum he had been granted, but nothing comprehensible issued forth.

Following the royal procession, a moment's silence was held in honour of Sir Henry Cecil. The queen herself led the mark of respect for the legendary trainer, who had sadly passed away, aged seventy, on the previous Tuesday. Her Majesty couldn't refrain from giving some thought to life's puzzling coincidences, for on the same day Prince Philip had been unwell – although not so dramatically to rule out the possibility of a quick recovery – Cecil had crossed the great divide instead.

'Sir Henry was an intrinsic part of Royal Ascot, with seventy-five winners over more than four decades,' said Johnny Weatherby, the queen's spokesman.

On the bright side, the Queen Anne Stakes was won by eight-to-one Declaration Of War, in a last-furlong sprint that propelled him ahead of the group on the pitch-perfect, smooth-as-a-billiard-table turf, earning Ritchie and Artan a nifty eighty quid each. The Kosovar was getting the hang of winning, whilst Ritchie could not believe his luck, money was coming in at long last. He pulled off a celebratory swinging orbit on his sticks even as his friend stooped forward and clapped joyously for him.

On Thursday Her Majesty, too, celebrated a thrilling victory in the Gold Cup, as her four-year-old filly, Estimate, despite being strongly challenged inside the final furlong by Simenon and Top Trip, stretched out her neck pluckily to cross the finish line first. Queen Elizabeth, snugly ensconced in the royal box in purple dress and hat, could hardly contain her excitement, she flashed the widest smile, her twinkling eyes narrowed in the oval frames of the notoriously oversized glasses, whereas John Warren, her racing adviser, having vigorously yelled himself hoarse for Estimate all the way to the end, now turned toward Her Majesty, clenching his fists in the air and taking his hat off to her.

For once, everyone was a winner. Who knows, it must be the whiff of summer sweetening the air, the extended hours of sunlight – despite the omnipresent veil of clouds fighting off the balmy rays and reminding everybody that this was England after all, and sun must be soaked up in small doses, lest it should go to one's head – but a prodigious, unforeseen happiness was brewing.

Day five was hectic, to say the least. There were six races throughout the afternoon, Idriz and Edonis joined the party, and so did Uncle Tariq and Grandpa Andri. The Chinaman was there, too, shooing away bad luck with his beaded mala bracelet, dangling and swaying it before him. Ritchie reinvested twenty of the eighty quid won on Tuesday in an each way accumulator that yielded no winners, but was good enough to return two hundred ninety-two pounds ninety-six pence. Life was definitely looking up.

On Monday morning, when he doddered into the first floor office of Kilburn jobcentre, aided by the left crutch only, the Indian lady at the signing point informed Ritchie that the manager would soon speak to him. 'Can you take a seat and wait please?'

Shortly afterwards Anoushka materialised from behind a partition, where she must have been busy sorting the fates of the nation's unemployed, and calling out his name met him at an empty desk right at the bottom of the room.

'As you have been informed already, you will be transferred to Willesden Green jobcentre, which is the closest to your postcode. Any problem with that?'

'No problem, thanks,' Ritchie said.

Anoushka picked up the phone and dialled the number of the office just mentioned to fix an appointment for him. She scribbled down the details on a slip of paper bearing the rectangular, green logo of the jobcentre, plus telephone and fax numbers and address.

'You have an appointment on Wednesday,' she said when she had put down the phone, squeezing her enormous breasts, scarcely fettered by the floral dress, between her arms, as she laid both elbows down on the desktop, squinting at him through the red-frame glasses with much circumspection. 'They will take care of you.'

Ritchie folded and pocketed the note, got to his feet, wrapped his left hand around the grip of the crutch and, about-facing, with unsteady gait, began his walk of shame past settees, partition screens, employees' desks and security attendants. There was no Williamson to see him off – he had vanished, nothing was left of him but a faint reminiscence of his exceptional girth and the tedious drone of his toneless voice still humming in Ritchie's ear – nor anybody else for that matter. Years of fortnightly attendance had been wiped out with a single gesture, an impersonal phone call, the national insurance number spelled out in a hurried frenzy, and off you go, nice to have met you, good bye and good luck.

'How is your foot?' asked Janet Barker in the evening, on the phone.

'Still hurting mum,' he replied, 'but it's not the end of the world, I will survive.'

'Josh is running a high fever again!'

'How come, the ginger is not working?'

'Nope.'

'I am sorry about that.'

On Wednesday Ritchie limped into Willesden jobcentre, delivered his claim form to a black lady on the ground floor, was told to show up again in two weeks' time for the eagerly awaited ceremony of the signature, then hopped back home. However, the routinely back and forth was not to be endured much longer. In fact, he was strongly advised to claim a different type of benefits from now on, the Employment and Support Allowance, which, given his poorly condition, would be much more befitting, entitling him to stay home for as long as there would be no improvements in his mobility.

Ritchie was assailed by a wistful sadness, the weight of survival on the breadline threatened to drag him down to eternal perdition. Once all the phone calls had been made though, and he found himself convalescent, but rid of the temporal afflictions of a life of daily struggles, he reflected if this wasn't, after all, a decisive step toward the ultimate goal of the Buddhist path. Wasn't this, perhaps, the Western equivalent of the accomplishment of that absence of activity of the mind, the elimination of desire, and the freedom from negative mental states that only one word could epitomize: nirvana? No suffering, no death could tear him away from it, he sensed. His rebirth was now complete.